DON'T READ THIS BOOK

13 FORBIDDEN TALES FROM THE MAD CITY

EDITED BY
CHUCK WENDIG

BASED ON THE WORLD OF
DON'T REST YOUR HEAD BY
FRED HICKS

An Evil Hat Productions Publication
www.evilhat.com
feedback@evilhat.com

First published in 2012 by Evil Hat Productions

Editor: Chuck Wendig
Art: George Cotronis
Design: Fred Hicks

Softcover ISBN: 978-1-61317-012-0
Kindle ISBN: 978-1-61317-013-7
ePub ISBN: 978-1-61317-014-4
iBooks ISBN: 978-1-61317-015-1

Printed in the USA

This is a work of fiction. All the characters and events
portrayed in this work are fictional. Any resemblance
to real people, events, dreams, figments, or nightmares
is purely coincidental. Keep telling yourself that.

CONTENTS

FOREWORD

BY FRED HICKS

I REMEMBER THE NIGHTMARE THAT STARTED IT ALL. I was running across a rooftop crammed with too many doorways and not enough exits. The city around me was familiar and strange, a mix of sooty Victorian architecture and cold modern glass. The thing chasing me was thick-featured and broad-shouldered. It moved woodenly, like a man built out of spare parts.

Later, I'd describe him as Frankenstein's monster, but that was just an attempt to put an easy label on an alien creature, to shake the unshakeable dream and assure myself that none of it was real.

Then, that same week, came the broadcast.

The radio told me about a military experiment. Soldiers given drugs were able to stay awake for days at a time, feeling none of the side effects of sleep deprivation—but if they stayed awake too long, their bodies and minds simply couldn't take it, and they'd die.

At least, that's how I remember the story, and it left me with questions. *What about the ones who didn't die? What, then, did they see?*

Somehow I knew my dream of the rooftops and monsters, the endless city built out of lost places and the creatures made of spare parts, was the answer. It was the Mad City, where nightmares walk the streets, and only those who are truly Awake could see what lies behind our familiar, comfortable, slumbering reality. They're changed by that knowledge. The Mad City seeps into them, makes them terrible and wild and desperate and just a little bit touched by its power. In their growing madness, the Awake teeter on the edge of becoming nightmares themselves—if they can avoid ending up on a dinner plate, of course.

Somehow, I'd seen through to that place, and it haunted me. I was rarely one to sleep easy. Had I become Awake? Were the nightmares looking up from their grisly meals at the sound of the dinner bell ringing once more?

I wrapped up my sense of unease, my admixture of anxiety and hope, in a neat little package called DON'T REST YOUR HEAD. A game. I had no real thought to put it out in the world, but it wanted to be seen, and so I made it happen.

Others read it, blended their own nightmares with mine. Told new impossible stories. The Mad City grew with the telling. Changed, grew strange, stayed familiar. Like the dream. Like the monster.

This nightmare was here to stay.

It doesn't have to be like that for you. Don't read this book. Look away, sleep well, and go on certain that the nightmares aren't real, certain that you're in no danger of becoming one yourself. That would be the comfortable thing to do. The safe thing.

Or, you can read on. Let them crawl into your skull, like they have into mine. Have them bang around until the noise makes it impossible to sleep. Until you have to stay Awake, and begin your descent into insomnia and madness.

Your choice.

Mine is already made.

DON'T LOSE YOUR PATIENTS

BY STEPHEN BLACKMOORE

THEY BRING HIM IN ON A 5150. Involuntary psych hold.

He's a weird one. Wide eyes, frothing at the mouth. Suit and a tie, but he smells like he's been living under the freeway.

"What's his name?" Carmichael asks, stuffing his stethoscope into his lab coat pocket, watching the man thrash on the bed as far in the back of the ER as the orderlies can stash him. The restraints are keeping him secured, but he's making people nervous.

"John Doe," the paramedic says. Big man. Has an ice pack pressed against a shiner on his right eye.

"He do that?"

The paramedic nods. "Yeah. Head-butt. Cops had him on the ground and zip-tied, but, you know." He shrugs.

Yeah, Carmichael thinks. Been there. "Any idea what he's on?"

"He won't say. Blood pressure was 170 over 110, pulse 140. Like a fucking jackhammer. Pupils are fine, though. To be honest, I don't think he's on anything. I think he's just freaked out."

"About what?"

"Keeps talking about nightmares."

"Seriously?"

"Yeah. Some boogeyman. I don't know." He twirls a finger around his ear, gives a low whistle. "Crazy."

Carmichael waits for the paramedic to leave before he pops another Adderall. He looks over at John Doe watching him dry swallow the pill. A grin slowly creeps across the man's face. He nods at Carmichael like he knows what he's going through.

Who knows, maybe he does.

Carmichael hasn't slept in five days. A month ago he thought it was just overwork keeping him up. So he just worked out harder, more time at the dojo. Left him exhausted, but every time he tried to sleep he'd bolt upright from the dreams.

Six hours of sleep turned into four, then three, then two. Now he stares at the television until it's time to come back to the hospital. At least in his emergency room he feels like he's accomplishing something.

Sleeping pills were a disaster. All those dreams and no chance to wake up from them.

He's running on Adderall, Modafinil, B-12 and caffeine. Takes him back to his med school days when he'd pop Benzedrine to get through tests, rotations, a second job.

He's starting to show the wear and the other doctors are starting to talk. But not too loudly. Not with a gang war going on and kids being wheeled in every night. Too many broken people and not enough doctors to fix them.

Carmichael is thinking about holes.

Big holes and small ones. Holes in society, holes in judgment. The holes people fall through and never return. Holes you can see and the holes you can't find.

The kid on the table can't be more than sixteen. Three gunshot wounds, perforated lung. Bleeding out faster than Carmichael can patch him up. Blood pressure dropping like Depression era stock.

Carmichael clamps and patches, resects and cauterizes, but he can't stop the bleeding because he can't find the hole.

Eighteen units of blood and it all ends up on the floor. It's no use. The kid spasms, flatlines. Dies.

Carmichael catches the kid's panicked eyes over the trach tube. Watches his dreams run out of him, his hopes drain away. All the things he could have been. Sports star, college grad, CEO. Father, brother, husband.

All because of a hole.

"You're Doctor Carmichael," John Doe says. He's still strapped down, but he's not thrashing. Carmichael had them push 8mg of Lorazepam into him. Should have knocked him flat. All it's done is mellow him out.

"And you're John Doe," Carmichael says.

He laughs. "Yes! I'm John Doe. Names are important, you know." He cocks his head in thought. "No, I guess you don't. Otherwise you'd be John Doe, too."

"Do you know why you're here?" I ask.

He ignores the question. "You have quite a few kids go through here," he says. "Weighs on you after a while, doesn't it? All that lost potential. All those broken dreams."

"It gets a little hairy from time to time," Carmichael says, wondering if he's been talking to himself where John Doe could overhear.

"Not sleeping much?" John Doe says. "Or at all. Dreams keeping you up, right. Hanging off you like Christmas ornaments. They're not even yours."

"I'm sorry?"

"The dreams," John Doe says. "They're not yours. They're the children's. The ones who come under your knife. They leave your table for a morgue drawer, but they leave their dreams behind. Somebody's got to take care of them. Might as well be you."

Carmichael is shaken. Tries to pull the conversation back to something he can handle.

"Police said you were taking a crowbar to a wall downtown."

"Couldn't find a hole," he says. "So I decided to make one. You know all about holes, don't you? Big ones, small ones. Holes you can see and the holes you can't find."

Carmichael stands up abruptly, rattled. "Somebody from Psych will be down to talk to you soon," he says.

"Gotcha, doc," John Doe says. "And thanks."

"For what?"

"The hole. I didn't know you had one here."

"Where's the guy in twelve?" the nurse says. Like all nurses at four in the morning she looks harried, in charge, not willing to take anybody's shit.

"Twelve?" Carmichael's been in surgery for the past two hours resecting someone's small intestine and he doesn't know what she's talking about.

"John Doe. He's being transferred to County, but he's not—"

Carmichael doesn't hear the rest. He runs to twelve, sees the empty bed, the open restraints. Tells the nurse behind him to check with security.

Carmichael doesn't know why he's so panicked. Not enough sleep. He's finally snapped. Maybe he needs to check into a psych ward himself. They get crazies in the hospital all the time. Why this one's so special Carmichael can't say.

But he knows he is.

It's stupid, and makes no sense because it's not like someone could fit under the bed, but he looks, anyway. That's when he sees light coming through a crack in the wall.

He shoves the bed aside, runs fingers along the crack of light. Digs in with his fingers and pulls out a section of wall a good three feet wide.

Behind it there's a hole.

The hole, John Doe had said. I didn't know you had one here.

Neither did Carmichael.

He turns to call out to the retreating nurse, tell her what he's found. But then something reaches from the hole, grabs him by the wrist and pulls.

Carmichael falls into a room that shouldn't be there. He lands hard on his back, knocking the air out of him. Images swim through his mind, flashes of dreams that don't feel right. Like they don't belong to him. And then they're gone, leaving only a memory that they existed, but not what they were.

At first he thinks John Doe has grabbed him. But then he realizes it's not a hand that has him by the wrist, but a tightly wrapped tentacle disappearing into a black, woolen sleeve.

The rest of his attacker looks like somebody tried to make a person and had nothing but soft wax and a mannequin to model it on. The eyes are drawn on in crude, fingerpaint swipes. Bright blue with spiky eyelashes going off in all directions. A thumb-drawn smile creases its half melted face.

Its proportions are almost right. Too thin, too tall. The black overcoat hangs on its frame like badly made doll clothing. A second tentacle peeks out of the other sleeve, whipping around like it's got a mind of its own.

And then the painted on smile splits open like a scalpel cut and Carmichael thinks he's staring into the mouth of a shark. Row upon row of needle teeth, lines of drool stretching between them. A thick, pox-scarred tongue slurps back and forth.

Carmichael gasps, tries to get air back into his deflated lungs. He takes a heaving breath, twists away from this monster, but it's no use. The tentacle on his wrist is reeling him in.

The thing's other tentacle whips Carmichael's face. He feels pain, a trickle of blood. Another flash of a memory he doesn't recognize that slips away like it's swirling down a drain. A sense of being somehow diminished.

He watches helpless as it raises its tentacle again. And as Carmichael thinks it's all over, that it will wrap that pale, ropy thing around his throat and squeeze, he feels the pressure on his wrist slacken. The thing gives a shudder. Falls to the floor.

John Doe pulls a large, wicked looking autopsy knife out of its back, the blade covered in thick, green goop. It's an antique. Like a breadknife in a lot of ways with a seven inch blade designed to cut through muscle and tendon instead of loaves of whole grain wheat.

He reaches down with his other hand and hauls Carmichael up.

"That first step's a real bastard," he says. "You okay?"

Carmichael's fallen into an operating theater, the equipment old and rusted, the glass of the observation room above him clouded and streaked with brown. The surgical lights affixed to the ceiling hang from broken joints, wires exposed, bulbs smashed. Water pools on the exposed concrete.

The hospital doesn't have a basement. It's all duct work and piping, access hatches and crawlspaces. None of this should be here. Not the operating room, not the equipment, not Carmichael.

And sure as hell not some Raggedy-Andy doll thing in a black overcoat with tentacles for hands.

"What the hell is that thing?" Carmichael asks. "And where the hell are we?"

John Doe wipes the knife on the thing's long black coat, leaving thick trails of ooze behind. "I've heard folks call them Harvesters. I've only seen a few of them. And only from a distance. Heard nasty stories about them, though. How are you doing?"

Carmichael looks at his wrist. It's ringed with a thick band of purple bruises where the tentacle wrapped around. He flexes his hand. He touches his face, expecting more blood, but it's just a thin line running down to his jaw. He probes at the wound, struck by the feeling that it's unusually small and incredibly large at the same time. He can't shake the feeling that he's lost something more precious than blood.

"A little sore but okay. And don't change the subject."

"I'm not," John Doe says. "You got lucky. With most people it slices them, bleeds them out and pumps them full of poison. And that's when they harvest."

Carmichael isn't sure he wants to know, but he asks anyway. "Harvest what?" Organs? Blood?

"Dreams."

Not the answer Carmichael is expecting, but something in the back of his mind, something in John Doe's tone tells him he's not lying.

"They'll suck the dreams right out of you," John Doe continues. "Then they take them back to their, hell I don't know what you'd call it. Lair, I guess." Joh Doe shudders. "Saw it once. Huge machines. They'll dump them in, pulp them down, sell them at the Bazaar."

"They sells dreams?"

"Oh, yeah," John Doe says. "Dreams, memories, fates. A good destiny will fetch you a pretty penny on the market." He raises a finger and pokes Carmichael in the chest. "And you, sir, are a walking gold mine."

"What do you mean?" Things have gone from strange to weird in only a few seconds. He rummages in his pockets, pulls out his stethoscope, a penlight. "I don't even have my wallet on me."

John Doe laughs. "Not cash, Doc. Come on. You know what I'm talking about."

They leave your table for a morgue drawer, but they leave their dreams behind. Somebody's got to take care of them. Might as well be you.

Part of him knows it's insane, tells him this isn't real, can't be happening. But that part clearly has missed the fact that it is standing in a broken down operating room that shouldn't exist with a dead, tentacled doll-monster and a man telling him that someone is harvesting dreams, so as far as Carmichaels' concerned that part can go fuck itself.

"Yes," Carmichael says. "I know what you're talking about."

"You'll need this."

John Doe hands him a chunk of rebar. He takes it, gives it an experimental swing. It's clumsy, unwieldy.

"What's this for?" Carmichael asks.

"Like I said, you're a gold mine. They're going to be hunting you down. First we get you out of this building," John Doe says. "Then we find you an exit."

Carmichael searches the ceiling for the way he came in but can find no sign of it.

"You won't find it," John Doe says.

"Sorry?"

"The hole," he says. "That's what you're looking for, right? They're all one way. The one that got you in, won't get you out. And vice versa."

"Do you know where one is?"

John Doe shrugs. "Everything moves around. But I'm more worried about getting out of the building."

"Where exactly are we?"

"You know those things you see out of the corner of your eye? Movement or a blotch you think is something but turns out to be nothing when you look right at it? That's this place. It's all in-between spaces and shoved into corners. A lot of people call it The Mad City, or just The City. One guy I know calls it Cleveland."

"And how come nobody knows about it?"

"Lots of people know about it. Just nobody anybody listens to. Hobos and fortune tellers and guys you strap onto gurneys and pump full of Ativan. Besides, you need to be special to see it at all."

"And I'm special?" Carmichael says.

"Just like Jerry's Kids."

They pick their way past broken doors, illuminating their way with Carmichael's penlight. The endless hallways are in even worse shape than the operating room. Open doorways, broken transoms.

Rusted lamps hang from the ceiling, their bulbs long ago burnt-out, broken or taken. Room numbers are scoured clean through age and disrepair. Offices are filled with junk and broken furniture.

Carmichael's seen photos of places like this before. Abandoned facilities in dead cities. Pripyat, Detroit. Evacuated desert towns with nothing left but the wind.

The floor above has collapsed into the hall. Carmichael looks up still expecting to see his hospital. They've been walking for so long that he doesn't know how this hallway would map to the real world. Or even if it does.

He stares at the space a long time looking for glimpses, trying to will it into being. But this world is too solid, and too insane to be brushed aside by things like hope.

"You all right?" John Doe says. His voice snaps Carmichael's attention from the rotting floor above. "You're breathing kinda hard there."

"Yeah," Carmichael says, scrubbing at his face with his hands. "No. I don't know."

None of this makes sense. There is a hospital here goddammit and it's not this torn out shell full of monsters. He grabs at that thought, that this isn't real, but all he gets hold of is vertigo, confusion, hopelessness.

"How long have you been here?" Carmichael says, trying to focus on something different. Something maybe he can get a handle on.

"About a year," John Doe says. "Maybe two. Time moves differently. Faster, slower. Hard to keep track."

"How'd you get here?" I say.

"Same as you," he says. "I got pulled."

"Is that how it works?"

He shrugs. "Not quite. We're what folks here call Awake. Lets us see things. Like the holes. I haven't slept since I got here."

"You haven't slept in a year?"

"Or two." The hallway stops in a T. "Right or left? Lady or the tiger?"

"Does it matter?" Carmichael says.

"Not really," he says. "Down here there's not much difference."

Carmichael leans down and checks the girl for a pulse, though he knows he won't find one.

At first they thought she was just another part of the debris piled up against the double doors, a discarded mannequin among rusted out medical equipment, broken beds, chairs and tables.

It's hard to tell how old she is, but she's young. Bloated, purple bruises around her throat and wrists, green fluid seeping out of her mouth. Rigor hasn't kicked in and when he rolls her over and checks her back he sees only splotches of red, not the wide patch of post-mortem lividity he'd expect on someone who had been dead a while.

"This happened recently," he says.

"Harvesters," John Doe says. "This is what happens when they take everything." He bends down to look at the body. "Looks like the tigers got the lady."

"This shouldn't happen," Carmichael says.

By the time they're done with their residency every doctor has seen someone die. And the dying always leave something behind. It's a palpable impression of vitality made clear by its absence. Death showing life as negative space. Footprints in sand.

But this violation is different. She's empty of life the way a statue is. Like she was never alive to begin with.

Rage bubbles in Carmichael's gut, crawls its way out. "No," he says.

"This is The City," John Doe says. "This happens all the time. You lose your dreams, you lose yourself. It's not like the real world is any different. How many dead kids do you see a night?"

Too many. Carmichael knows he's right, but out there he knows he can't do anything but patch them up and hope they don't come back in a body bag. But here? Dreams can be bought and sold. Octopus doll monsters wander abandoned hospitals murdering children.

He doesn't know how, but he knows that he has to end this.

Tracking The Harvester has proved surprisingly easy. The floors are covered in thick dust. Footprints, paw prints, the occasional line from a rat's tail disturbs it. But the freshest of these tracks are the wide brushstrokes of the Harvester's long, black coat.

They follow it through hallways that never seem to end, past burnt out patient rooms and offices.

Carmichael doesn't care about finding a hole that will get him back to the real world, anymore. Right now he wants one thing; that Harvester's head on a stick.

And somewhere down a flight of steps dropping down into darkness it's waiting for him.

"You really want to do this?" John Doe says.

Carmichael is having second thoughts. What's gotten into him? Anger, certainly. Frustration. But he feels driven.

"No, but I have to," he says.

John Doe laughs. It's a brittle sound that echoes off the walls. "Fair enough," he says. "This'll be easy."

"You sound very sure," Carmichael says.

"I'm an old hand at dealing with The City. It's dangerous, but I got your back."

Carmichael looks at John Doe's autopsy knife barely visible in the gloom then at the rebar in his own hand. For a moment, he's a little jealous, though he knows he has no reason to be. It's just how it worked out. A solid steel bar should be enough to cave in some impossible monster's head.

Carmichael's vision blurs for a moment. The exhaustion hitting him hard. He digs out another Adderall from his pocket. Offers one to John Doe, who just shakes his head.

"I don't need those, anymore," he says.

"How far do you think we've gone?" Carmichael asks as they continue down the stairs. Down here there are no lights. Just dark and more dark.

"Five stories?" John Doe says. "Six?"

They continue walking in silence. Another floor down and the darkness grows. Carmichael's groping the walls, testing each step with a careful foot.

"You're a good man," John Doe says behind him, his voice startlingly close. "I'm really sorry for this."

"Hey, you didn't pull me in here."

John Doe says nothing for a long time and Carmichael wonders for a moment if he's slipped away in the darkness. Then, "That's not what I'm sorry for."

Carmichael feels a sharp pain at the base of his skull. His vision flares, vertigo pulling him down. He staggers, lashes out with the re-bar, doesn't connect. Another blow, and another. He falls to his knees, flailing. Wonders why John Doe isn't helping him.

Figures it out a minute too late.

Carmichael wakes to jarring thuds and too bright lights that burn through his eyelids. He opens an eye against the pain, watches the lights flash by overhead. He's strapped to a gurney being wheeled down a corridor. At first there's relief. He's back in the hospital. He's fallen and hit his head in the emergency room and they're taking him back to check on him.

All that Harvester business was just a hallucination, a side effect of his concussion.

But then he turns his head to look around him and he realizes it's not.

This hallway is in better shape than the others, with some lights still functioning, but the floor is littered with trash that the gurney clatters over, sending new waves of nausea through him with each bump.

The rooms they pass have bricked over doorways. No attempts made to paint them. Under the sounds of the gurney's wheels and John Doe's huffing breath Carmichael hears whispers, muted cries. He wonders if anyone is still inside those rooms.

"What's happening?" Carmichael says. He can taste blood and feel it dried on the back of his head. He pulls against the leather straps holding him down. One of them shifts a bit, but doesn't give.

"Told ya, doc. You're a goldmine."

Carmichael can't quite get his thoughts in place. They slide along each other's surfaces like slick ice. "The Harvesters—"

"Fuck the Harvesters," John Doe says. He yanks the gurney to a stop, spins it around to stare into Carmichael's face. "There's worse down here than Harvesters."

"Like you?" Carmichael's head is clearing and confusion is shifting to anger. Rage pushes aside the pain, the double vision. He strains against his bonds again, that one strap loosening a bit more.

John Doe laughs. "I wish. No, worse than me. That's why I need you, doc. Need a stake if I want to make it down here. You're my ticket to the big time."

"You want the dreams," Carmichael says. He's still having trouble believing that they can be a living thing, something you can hold in your hand.

"Well, duh. You know, I've been hunting you down for weeks. Not you, exactly. Someone like you. Do you know how hard it is to find somebody who hangs onto shit the way you do? I tried orphanages, jails, funeral homes. Nada. You are one seriously maladjusted motherfucker, doc. You really should try therapy."

John Doe spins the gurney again. Carmichael has to fight to keep from throwing up as John Doe starts pushing him further down the hall.

The hallway ends in a set of double doors, wired glass windows painted over. Light streams through the door's edges. Carmichael can smell decay and rot, the thick stink of blood. An undercurrent of smoke and oil. The sound of pumps and mechanical hissing is loud in his ears.

"There are more Harvesters in there," John Doe says, squinting at the doors as though they're a math problem. "I don't suppose you'd help me fight them, would you?" He looks over his shoulder at Carmichael.

Carmichael would love to tell him what he thinks of that idea but he's got a filthy rag shoved into his mouth and the only sound that comes out is a muted grunt.

"No," John Doe says, "I didn't think so."

He gets behind the gurney. Carmichael cranes his head to watch him. That one loose strap has gotten looser, all his wriggling beginning to pay off, but Carmichael needs more time. A few seconds, maybe. A minute at most.

John Doe squares his shoulders. "Might as well get this over with."

He shoves the gurney, screaming like a mad jackal as he breaks through the doors. Once the gurney clears he lets go. All Carmichael can see is bright lights, a hint of steel and brass equipment. The gurney flies across the room, wobbles, spins. Tips up on two wheels, flips over.

He hits the muck covered floor, slides through a thin sheen of charnel house waste. The gurney finally stops when it slams against a large brass tank with hoses spouting hoses like an octopus, each one spreading across the floor to other tanks and devices arranged throughout the room. He gives it all a cursory glance, ignoring the Harvesters tending levers and gauges as he yanks the straps off.

John Doe is running around the room shrieking. The two Harvesters in the room have left their stations to converge on him. Carmichael is torn between three options; running away, helping John Doe kill the Harvesters, or helping the Harvesters kill John Doe.

Then he sees the victims. On one side of the room sit a dozen filthy hospital beds, each one holding a strapped-in body. All of them pierced through with clear hoses siphoning a gold fluid. Men, women, children. Some of them move, most don't. He's not sure how many are alive.

So he chooses option four.

While John Doe and the Harvesters go at it, Carmichael runs to the abandoned equipment and starts throwing every lever he can find to the off position. He doesn't know if this will help, hinder or even kill these people, but dammit he can't think of what else to do. As he shuts things down a low rumble starts to develop in the brass tank. The hoses stop draining, the pumps stop pumping.

He has everyone's attention.

He turns to John Doe and the two Harvesters. As the Harvesters lope toward him John Doe takes advantage of the distraction to run one through with that nasty autopsy blade. The other is on Carmichael in a flash.

He ducks beneath a tentacle, but he's too slow to avoid the other. It hits him, wrapping around his neck like a bullwhip. He has that same feeling of thoughts and memories being sucked out of him that he had the first time a Harvester hit him.

When the dreams go, they're gone and he can only remember that they existed, but not what they were.

The Harvester splits open its painted on smile. It bends its head down to Carmichael's face. If it doesn't strangle him it will just bite his head off.

Carmichael knew this was a gamble. It's not like he went into this with a great plan. But he's pretty sure he's got John Doe figured out.

Sure enough, the Harvester shudders as the autopsy blade punches through. It shudders, slackens. Falls on top of Carmichael.

John Doe half pulls the Harvester off as the room fills with the sounds of boilers going critical, pipes about to burst. His face is pure panic. He grabs Carmichael by the shirt. "What have you done?"

"You need this, don't you?" Carmichael yells over the increasing noise. "You can't do what they do, so you need this equipment."

John Doe drops Carmichael. He's grabbing hanks of his hair in frustration, muttering, "No, no, no," over and over again. He runs to the vibrating brass tank. Rivets pop, liquid sprays through buckling seams.

The tank explodes into shrapnel, shredding John Doe with a thousand flying pieces. Carmichael, half beneath the Harvester's body, is shielded from the worst of it. Metal tears into an exposed leg.

The tank's contents spray across the room, bathing everything in viscous foam. When it showers Carmichael a million images burst in on him, soaking into his mind as surely as it's soaking into his clothes.

Between the pain, the concussion and the overwhelming onslaught of dreams, Carmichael can't take it. He slumps unconscious to the floor.

"Are you dead?"

Carmichael cracks open an eye. He's lying in a soup of filthy liquid. A child with dull eyes stands over him. He's covered in scabbed-over wounds and punctures still welling with drying blood.

"I'm not dead." Dead wouldn't hurt this much. His head is throbbing, his leg is on fire.

"Did you kill them?" the boy asks.

"Sort of."

"Thanks."

Carmichael sits up, shoves the dead Harvester off. Its back is riddled with brass slivers. Likewise Carmichael's leg. Most of the damage is superficial, but he knows he'll need stitches.

He starts to stand, the kid reaching out to help him. When they touch Carmichael feels like somebody's nailed him with a cattle prod. Images of life in the City flare through him. Rooftops, flying, running from strange clockwork men. Dreams of safety, nightmares of being chased.

It's like when the Harvesters hit him, only instead of a feeling of being sucked dry, it's a sense of returning something that doesn't belong to him.

The kid goes rigid and for a moment Carmichael's scared he's hurt him. But then it passes and there's something different. The dullness in his eyes fades, a smile quirks up at the corners of his mouth.

"You all right?" he asks the kid, bending down on his good leg to look him over.

"Yeah," the kid says. "I think so." He looks over his shoulders at the tumbled down row of beds, scattered by the blast. "I think some of them might need help."

Carmichael looks at the bodies, some of them still moving. The shrapnel either didn't get that far or it was absorbed by the equipment they were hooked to. He gets up, hobbles to them. Some are dead. The living all have that dull, empty look in their eyes.

Carmichael looks at his hands, looks at the confused, empty faces. Maybe this is why he's here. He bends down to a girl lying on the floor.

He doesn't know, but maybe it's time to find out.

STEPHEN BLACKMOORE is the author of the paranormal noir novel *City Of The Lost* through DAW Books. His short stories have appeared in anthologies and magazines such as *Uncage Me, Deadly Treats, Plots With Guns* and *Crime Factory.* He is an editor of the noir magazine *Needle* and is an all around swell guy. Really. Just ask anyone. Except that guy down the street. He's stinky.

You can reach Stephen through his website:

http://stephenblackmoore.com

DON'T BE YOUR FATHER

BY RICHARD DANSKY

THE THING THAT KEPT DADDY UP NIGHTS was me.

There was a monster under the bed, you see. I was sure of it. Every night, I'd hear it moving around. I'd hear its breathing, raspy and low, like an old man who'd washed gravel down with whisky, and smoked cigarettes laced with glass. I'd hear its voice, muttering that it would be there, that it would always be there, and that nothing was ever going to take it away.

Sometimes, I'd even feel it bang up against the underside of my boxspring and I'd know, I'd just know there was something impossibly large down there. Alert. Alive.

Waiting.

And then I'd start screaming, and Daddy would come pounding up the stairs like the hero he wanted to be for me. He'd throw the door open and he'd ask me if I was all right. He knew the answer, of course. He'd come running up those stairs the night before, and the night before that, and every night for months. Mom slept through it. She was sick, the doctors said. Needed her medicine to make sure she slept through the night. So it was Daddy who heard, and Daddy who came running, and Daddy who snatched a couple of hours of sleep here and there between the screams.

Eventually, he stopped sleeping. He just sat at the kitchen table with a cup of coffee and a burial mound of cigarette butts, waiting.

One night, he stopped waiting. One night he went away.

It's three thirty in the morning, give or take the duration of a quick piss up against an alley wall. The alley's one I've never been down, off a street I've never seen, in a neighborhood I've never known. I grew up in this city, and I've never been as lost as I am now.

I zip up my pants and look up. The thin strip of sky visible overhead is purple with low-hanging clouds. They're moving fast, and every time I blink they're moving in a different direction. Crazy winds, I tell myself. Tornado weather. I look back down and my piss is flowing up the wall, spelling letters in an alphabet I've never seen before. It's familiar, though, close enough to understanding that I lean in little closer to get a better look, and—

"You want to smell your own whiz, you don't have to leave the house," says a voice from behind me, too close to mean well. I turn and I step back and I put my hands up into some kind of defensive gesture, and about the time the thing in front of me comes into focus I realize what a dumbass move I've made as the back of my shirt is suddenly soaked.

The man in front of me, who was the man behind me, who was the man who wasn't there a minute ago, is tall. He's wearing a brown trenchcoat and a brown leather hat that shadows his face, and brown leather gloves on his hands. The brim of his hat hides his face, and his gloves hide his hands, and there's nothing I can see of him that isn't cowhide.

"Stay back, pal," I tell him, but I can see he isn't impressed. He laughs instead, and he holds up both hands to show he's not holding a knife or a gun, and I see that they're not gloves he's wearing, they're mittens. Flat, square mittens with no thumbs, and then he tilts his head up so that the streetlight catches what's underneath, the flapping mouth and the empty eyes, and my throat's too tight to scream.

The door slams and Daddy's gone, and I'm the only one who knows. I'm awake because there's a monster under the bed, and now Daddy's gone and no one can protect me. He's gone out before in the middle of the night, midnight runs for more coffee or more cigarettes or, once in a while, a bottle of something in a plain brown paper bag. All these things I have heard, and I know what the door sounds like when Daddy's just going out for a minute.

This time, the door closes and it sounds like Daddy's gone forever. Mom doesn't hear it. She's asleep. She'll always be asleep. She can't protect me. I'm the only one who hears it. I'm the only one who hears that Daddy's gone forever, and he isn't coming back.

Underneath the bed, the monster stirs.

Widdershingles. That's where the man made of empty wallets and lost dreams tells me to go. "Up," he says. "That's where the lost fathers always go."

"Why," I ask him. I do not understand where this man, this thing has come from. I do not understand how it can exist. But deep down, a part of me knows that he is the one who belongs here in this part of town I've never seen, that here he's the natural and ordinary one, and I'm the trespasser.

I don't ask him what he calls this neighborhood, or this city. I'm afraid he might answer.

"Stars," he says, and points one flapping wallet-hand up at that boiling rope of purple sky. "They want to see the stars and tell themselves those are the same stars their kids are looking at back home, back in the waking world."

"And are they?" I ask.

He cocks his head at me. I hear a rustle of leather as he grins. "Naw," he says. "Stars are something else here. But you gotta watch 'em try." He blinks, wallet-eyes slapping open and shut. "You got any kids?"

"One," I tell him without understanding why. "A daughter. She's.... she's having nightmares." And then I clamp my lips down, and don't tell him about the screaming, about the bad dreams, about the stories of the monster under the bed that whispers to her every night.

"Ah. Get home to her, if you can. But first," and he jerked one squared-off hand at a fire escape. "Go up. Look at the stars. Your dad might have looked at the same ones."

He laughs then, an ugly, slapping sound, and then dissolves into a pile of discarded wallets on the street. I stare at it and they suddenly take flight, a whirling cloud of flapping, leathery wings that circle around me before vanishing up into the night.

Daddy didn't come back, not that I blame him. Mom did, and Mom blamed me for making him leave. And when I told her about the monster, she gave me some of her medicine, so I would sleep, too.

"But then the monster will get me," I told her.

"But you'll be asleep," she said. "And you'll never know."

By the time I hit the rooftop, my hands are bloody. The fire escape is old and rusted, jagged in precisely the places where hands are supposed to go, and I tell myself that if I ever get out of this place, I'm getting a tetanus shot. The back of my shirt has dried and then soaked through again, piss and sweat in salty stinking combination. I'm going to have to throw the shirt out when I get home, which is a shame. It's got an image of Grumpy the Dwarf on it, and my daughter loves it. She "bought" it for me, she and her mother, back before her mother left me, too.

The roof is flat, dotted with fans and vents and strange shapes belching out steam. It's covered in black gravel, and wadded-up newspapers blow across it in patterns that don't match the wind. Above me is the night sky, sliced in ribbons where stars do and don't shine. A few look familiar. Most don't. I wonder if my father stood on this safe rooftop, looked up at those same stars.

I wonder if he jumped.

I left home, too. Not like Daddy did. He disappeared; I went to college. Went as far away from home as I could and tried never to look back. Mom never asked me to come home, which was just as well. I wouldn't have gone. Instead, I made a new life—hard to be worried about the monster under the bed when you're in the top bunk of a freshman dorm. I turned myself into a new person. Studied hard, did well, graduated and got a job and a girl and a life and—

—and one night, my daughter, the most important thing in my life, woke up screaming.

More newspapers are scudding around on the roof now than when I first climbed up here. The wind's been blowing them up the sides of the building, and as they reach the top, they roll together like tumbleweeds. For a moment, I watch them, fascinated, and then I realize there's no wind up here. The newspapers are unfolding themselves now, joining themselves into bigger shapes, ones that are vaguely humanoid. On their flat, front-page faces I can see the hints of stories, pictures and names in big block type. "LOCAL MAN DISAPPEARS", one says. "DEADBEAT DAD FOUND—SAYS HE'S HAPPY HE LEFT HIS BRAT BEHIND" reads another. "WOMAN MURDERS ABUSIVE HUSBAND" says a third, and the picture that's coming into focus is too familiar.

"No!" The word tears itself out of me and I turn. I run, and the rustle of paper, follows me. They've got voices now, these paperboys, thin and reedy and mocking, and getting louder with each step.

I reach the edge of the roof. It's thirty feet down to the street, and maybe ten across to the next building. The catcalls are getting louder, "Who was the real monster?" and "Why did your daddy leave?" and "Breaking news, you're gonna disappear, too!"

I don't look back. I don't slow down. I jump...

We stuck it out for a few months once the screaming started. We took my daughter to a child psychiatrist, we changed her room, we did everything we could. On the nights when my wife watched her, she was fine. On the nights when I did, or no one else was in the room, screaming. Terror. And, ultimately, the end of the marriage.

Nobody came out and said that I'd abused my daughter. I hadn't, for one thing. There was no proof I had, for another. But the fact that she woke up howling on the nights when her mother wasn't there got people thinking.

I should have moved out. Come to think of it, I should have known not to have kids. And I should have known that telling my wife—my ex-wife—about what happened when I was growing up, the real truth of it, was a bad idea.

That's what finally made her leave. That's what made her take my daughter with her.

And me, I moved back home. Because really, what else was I going to do?

I soar across the gap between buildings, legs and arms windmilling all the way. My gut hits the edge of a rooftop, and I fold myself over it to safety. A quick scrabble drags my legs up, and then I'm running again. The hoots and hollers have gotten louder and more vicious, and I can hear more of them ahead of me. I'm being surrounded.

Across the rooftop I go. Dead ahead is another street, but the buildings to the left and right are level with mine. I pick left and go, sprinting like a madman.

This is insane, I tell myself. I've got to get out of here. I've got to get home. I've got to get to my daughter.

And behind me the loping newspaper men pick up speed.

It was the card that did it. The card came from my daughter, written in orange colored pencil. I'd gotten notes from her before, carefully packed by my ex-wife and filled with stories of what she was doing at school and how well she was feeling and how she and Mommy were having a great time together.

Occasionally, she even said she missed me.

This card was different. It wasn't in one of my ex-wife's lavender-scented envelopes. It didn't have parental approval. It came straight from my daughter. And it said, "There's something under my bed."

That was the last night of sleep I had.

Rooftop to rooftop. Jump down to the next building, dodge a paper man when he springs out from behind a ventilation duct, leap and pray I'll catch myself on a fire escape or window ledge or rooftop sprawl. I'm coughing now, each breath burning a line in my side. Too many cigarettes, I think. Too much booze once my daughter got taken away, and now my breathing is a raspy, wet thing. "Don't stop," I tell myself. "Gotta keep going," and the voice is familiar.

A newspaper man pops up in front of me, splaying his front page wide. The image is from my childhood; me in my pajamas, Daddy rearing back away from me. The headline reads "MY FATHER WAS A MONSTER!"

I reach out to shred it, to tear it to pieces but I'm too slow; he's too fast for me and he's ducked underneath my swing. His friends are coming by the dozens, and too late I realize I'm trapped, stopped dead. Maybe Daddy was a monster, I think. Maybe he didn't just go away. Maybe they took him—

"No!" The scream goes up to the heavens, to that weird uncaring sky, and I throw myself off the rooftop. My hands catch onto a drainpipe and I half-slide, half slip down the side of the building to the ground. The shock of landing stabs up through my knees, but I don't care. I'm off and running. More of the paper men are here, already in pursuit. I know what they want to show me—another version of that picture, with me and my daughter instead of Daddy and me. It's not true. it never was true. They'll make it true.

I run.

Sleep went away. I called my ex-wife and told her I wanted to come visit. She said that wasn't a good idea. So did her lawyer. I bought a plane ticket, cancelled it, bought another one, tore it up and stayed home. I had to go to her. I couldn't go to her. I had to protect her. If I tried to, my ex-wife would have me arrested. So I wrote her letters that I'm sure she never saw, and I sent her presents I don't know if she ever got, and I worried.

I don't sleep. I can't sleep.

And one night, I walk out the door just like Daddy did, and I find myself here.

They're still chasing me. I run down the rain-slick streets, and see more of them up ahead. Nowhere to go, nowhere to run. I cut down an alley to my left and they follow, whooping. Boxes topple behind me as I run, and then suddenly, I'm face to face with a brick wall. It's a dead end. The alley behind me is filling up. I've got nowhere to run. I look around, and then I see a door, set flush against the wall in the corner.

There's a lock on it, but I pick up a brick from the alley floor and bash it off. It comes away clean, then I throw the door open and run inside.

It's a cellar, narrow and mostly empty. I don't see any stairs up in the thin light that filters in from the alley; I do see the hatch to a crawlspace. It's the only way out. And I can hear footsteps behind me, so I tear the crawlspace door open and dive in.

It's narrow, and dark, and smells like burned dust and old spilled coffee. I have to hunch my shoulders up so that I can move forward, inchworming it as fast as I can. They're behind me. I can still hear them. I will not let them catch me. I will not let them turn me into the monster they want me to be. More dust fills the air now and I'm coughing, deep ragged sounds that don't sound like they're coming from a human throat. The corridor's getting narrower. I can't go back. They'll catch me if I go back. Something grabs at my feet and I kick it away, and then it's a turn and I have to twist and I can see a thin line of light in the distance.

Got to keep going, I tell myself. Can't disappear from my daughter's life. Can't do to her what was done to me.

The light's getting closer. Something's blocking a segment of it, a dark shape with fuzzy edges. Don't care. Got to get out. Can't stop coughing. Got to keep going. All twisted up now, don't care. Don't care what happens to me, just have to get out, get to her, keep her safe.

And then the tunnel widens out, and I reach my hand out, my knotted, bloody, hand, and it closes around a stuffed animal.

A stuffed animal I gave my daughter.

And the light is the light under her bedroom door from the night-light we kept on in the hallway, to keep the monsters away.

And my breathing is a monstrous rasp, and I can hear a voice that I don't recognize as mine muttering about how he has to find her, has to protect her.

And above me, in the bed, my little girl starts screaming.

The Central Clancy Writer for Ubisoft/Red Storm, **RICHARD DANSKY** was named one of the Top 20 videogame writers by Gamasutra in 2009. He's also been using that tidbit in his bios ever since, as well as mentioning novels like *Firefly Rain,* videogames like *Splinter Cell: Conviction,* and the hundred-plus projects he contributed to back when he was working for White Wolf as the line developer for *Wraith: The Oblivion.* He lives in North Carolina with his wife, their inevitable cats, and the ghost of a zombie frog.

DON'T WRECK YOUR SOUL

BY C.E. MURPHY

MY SISTER AMALEE KILLED HERSELF the second Friday of Lent. She'd given up sex and said she couldn't take it any more, but that's crap. Nobody kills themselves over breaking a Lenten vow. At worst that's a venial sin, and suicide is a mortal one. Anyway, no, she didn't kill herself over sex, no matter what the note said.

She killed herself because of the nightmares.

I know, because they came to me when she was gone.

Everybody has nightmares. The same stupid dream that doesn't make any sense, like realizing you've skipped class all semester and now there's a final exam you're totally unprepared for. Or the one where something's after you and the fastest you can run is super-slow, or the one where you're slipping down an icy crevasse and the snow is piling up over your head and you can't breathe can't move can't scrabble free every time somebody tries to help you get buried deeper it's cold your heart is bursting you know it can't be real it's a dream but if I'm dreaming and I realize it then I'm supposed to wake up oh Jesus I'm *not* dreaming because I didn't wake up I'm really buried alive oh God please no I'm going to *die—*

Here's the thing, though: those nightmares come in your *sleep*.

Amalee's came while she was awake. She never ever slept, not if she could help it. She drank that gross-smelling Blood of the Bull energy drink and popped the caffeine pills until she jittered and I used to laugh at her, until she killed herself and then I couldn't sleep either.

And now I talk to the Devil in my still-awake-dreams, and he's offering me a chance to bring Amalee back from the dead.

He comes to me every night, when I'm staring at the city-gone-mad. I see things in it I never saw before, wraiths and demons and dancers in the dust. I don't know if they're beautiful or terrible, with their pixelated edges made of light and their gazes as hollow as a starless night. I walk through them every night and they touch me, exquisite pain on my skin, like rolling in shattered crystal. My eyes bleed, tears of blood like a vampire cries, but I can't, don't want to, look away.

I should, I know I should, because I've been told forever, my mother likes to use that line from the old movie, *never dance with the devil in the pale moonlight*, but my mother never saw the Devil when he asked her to dance. Me, he's walking right next to me, his step in time with mine, and what they don't want to tell you in Bible Studies is that he's beautiful. They tell you he was Lucifer, the Morning Star, most beloved angel of God, but they make him red-faced and horned and with forked tail, and it's a lie. Even fallen, he's radiant. Black-haired, blue-eyed, a smile like sun rising on the horizon. *Bring her back*, he whispers. *We can bring her back.*

I try not to look as he crosses the church's threshold with me. The priests say he shouldn't be able to, but they say he can quote Scripture for his own purposes, too, so maybe he's the man on the pulpit and they're the devils themselves.

No. That kind of thinking won't help. I kneel to pray, not on one of the padded pews but the other ones, the ones that the old and the faithful and the more-pious-than-thou use, because they think they're better than you are, or maybe they think God listens harder if your knees hurt. Just in case I kneel there too, and lock my hands together in prayer. They're cold, almost as cold as Amalee was when I found her. Her eyes were open and staring, tear tracks standing out white against already-white skin, but her mouth was smiling. Not joy, but relief. I knew why now. No more nightmares.

The Devil puts his warm hands over mine and I melt inside. He'll keep the cold away, he'll keep memories and dreams away. All I have to do is stay awake. Keep moving forward, keep praying, keep *not thinking* about the last time I saw Amalee alive—O *Father who art in Heaven, hallowed be thy name*—

Thy kingdom come, says the Devil in my mind. *Thy will be done. She can live again. You know it's in you. Rise up and walk with the Lord on Earth as it is in Heaven.*

That's crazy talk, and I hate the creeping feeling along my spine that it's true. The city beyond the church has gone mad, and it's taking me with it. It's making me think I can raise the dead. If I could just sleep these thoughts would go away.

But so would he, my beautiful Devil, so bright I can see him with my eyes closed. He's earnest and solemn and his voice is incessant in my head: *she can rise like Christ rose, did you never wonder how that came to be? God, yes, but God works in mysterious ways. Don't you think God walks the streets of the City Slumbering? Don't you know that's how He finds those who can be Awakened? You're Awake now. Don't be afraid of what it means. Bring Amalee back. Say you're sorry, so you can be forgiven.*

I pull my hands from his and run. Run like I do in dreams, too slowly, with the Devil on my heels. Run from him, run from the things I said to Amalee, the things that keep me awake so long that nightmares come when my eyes are still open, *you're a slut, God doesn't love you, I don't love you, Mom and Dad don't love you.* Run from judgment, lest I be judged.

The Devil is waiting for me when I stop running. It doesn't matter where I go, he's there, smiling, ready to embrace me the way God won't have embraced Amalee because she killed herself and He might love sluts but He can't forgive a suicide. It's hard not to run straight into the Devil's arms when I know my sister's sleeping with him now.

He's holding a dead thing. A bird, a rat, a dog, a cat. Something small and limp and I don't want to see. *Just try it,* he says. *Let it flow through you, the power of life. The power over death. A little thing like this doesn't deserve to die, does it?*

Of course it doesn't, screw the natural order, nobody, nothing should die. Nothing but mosquitoes and spiders, anyway, even if that would mess up the natural order too and it's a kitten in the Devil's hands, how can anybody kill a kitten. I make a sad sound and touch it without meaning to, without wanting to, and I wish it wasn't dead.

And if wishes were fishes we'd all eat like kings, but something happens, something terrible and wonderful that starts in my core and splashes two ways. Splashes up, like God rising in me, warm and gentle and alive.

Splashes down, hot and quick and sweet between my legs so that I stagger and blush with the rush of pleasure.

And under my fingertips the sex feeling comes to life in the kitten, bright and beautiful and fresh and new. Breath fills its body and it meeps a tiny surprised sound, then leaps down and runs away purring.

My knees quit working and I fall to them, watching a patch of calico scurry into the mad city. Alive. Adorable. Impossible. I think *I have a gift*, and the hot rush happens again, leaving me trembling with excitement and wanting more. I look up.

For half a second I think the Devil's face has gone crazy, a million screams breaking through. He's distorted, exultant, triumphant, terrible. Then I blink and it's all gone, his sweet smile back in place and his hands open to mine. He draws me up and draws me in. His hands stroke my spine until the heat inside me becomes unbearable. *That's the Devil*, part of me thinks. *Hellfire and brimstone. That's why I'm so hot.* But hellfire and brimstone should hurt, and the only hurt here is from the pounding need for more.

And then I think if saving the kitten felt so good how much better will saving my sister feel? Maybe the white-hot pulse will never end, if I bring another human being back from the dead. And that seems worth it, seems smart, seems good, and besides then I'll have my sister back, so I walk with the Devil in the pale moonlight, and we pass by a thousand tired faces in the crazy bad city.

One is a little girl, and she's awake, Awake like I am. Her eyes are burned holes in her head and her hands writhe with power bigger than she is. It wants out, that power, and it's eating its way through her. It's not a good gift, not like the one I have. It just wants to be free, and doesn't care if it kills the little girl to get that way.

I stop.

The Devil tugs me on. I shake my head and lock my knees. I can't take my eyes off the little girl, and the heat inside me is building again. I don't know what the girl can do with her magic, what good it is, maybe there isn't any good in it, maybe it's just going to kill her, but I just said to the Devil that nothing deserves to die, or maybe he said it to me but never mind anyway I unlock my knees and go to the girl even as the Devil drags me back. *No,* he says, *no, you won't get what you want, what you need, this way. Listen to me, trust me, let me show you—*

But I'm not listening, not right now, not with the hot want inside me and the Devil's words ringing in my mind: *nothing deserves to die.*

I touch the little girl's hair like I touched the kitten's fur, and the hot rush happens again. Except this time it's *horrible.* It *stops,* all the sweetness and need ready to explode just *stops* like a light's been switched off, leaving my mind, my body, expecting the light and instead left wanting in the darkness.

The Devil's lip is curled, and he says *you see?* And I do, I see, I see that for the sweetness to explode inside me the way I want it to, I can't make living things better, only dead ones.

But the little girl is making light with her hands now, warmed by it instead of burning up from inside, and I see that too. I don't know how it happened, how the hot rush inside me turned to a controllable burn in the girl, but I'm sure it was me. I'm sure the smears of colored light she paints in the air, like long-exposure photography come to life, I'm sure I made that happen so she could release the crazy gift the way she wants to instead of having it burn through her and leave her dead on the side of the street. It was me, and if I could only think how I did it, I might understand—

The Devil pulls me closer and puts his mouth on my throat. I swallow, then whimper, and press myself all up against him. I want him to touch me places nobody ever has, not even me, so that the heat and sweetness comes back. It hurts that it stopped, even if the little girl is running away happy now, but that's in the past and the Devil is here beside me, with me, almost inside me, and he's starting to make the pain go away.

But I can't, he says, *I can't. Only you can do that. Only you can bring her back so the heat and sweet never end, so you can say you love her, so you can say you're sorry. Bring her back, so you can be mine. Come with me*, he says, *we'll find her and then the hot rush will never, ever go away.*

I say *yes* and a little promise of that pleasure erupts inside me. Then we're walking again, the Devil's hand hot in mine. Walking, striding, scurrying, hurrying, running to the graveyard, where the Devil makes me dig. Fingernails and fistsful of dirt, loose-packed earth because it hasn't had time to collapse. It takes forever to unbury my sister, and I'm filthy and stinking by the time I pry her coffin open.

She is perfect, as beautiful as she was the day we buried her. She lies in hallowed ground even though we know God wouldn't take her soul, because it was easier for us to put her here and the priest looked the other way. *An accident*, he said, *a terrible accident*, though how anybody *accidents* long bloody lines up their inner arms and across their wrists I don't know. But *an accident* lets us bury her in consecrated earth, holy earth from which I've excavated her now, and I haul her chemically-preserved body to the grass beside the grave, and the need inside me screams with excitement as I wrangle her dead body. I can do this, I have to do this, I *need* to do this.

I don't want to do this.

The Devil is sitting across from me, across from Amalee's body, and he's smiling. I want him to smile at me like that forever. I'm warm with the Morning Star, warmer than I've ever been. Burning in hellfire warm, but I don't care. Amalee is cold and dead and as long as she stays that way, nothing I ever do will unsay the things I said to her the morning that she died. I can say *I'm sorry, I'm sorry, I'm sorry* until the end of time and unless she hears me it won't undo the nightmares.

I can see their shape in the Devil's handsome face. Screaming laughing lusting mouths and eyes, hungry tongues and sly angry gazes. He is fracturing with them, his beauty barely containing them, and all they want me to do is take back my dead. All I want me to do is take her back, too, and when she breathes again, ask for forgiveness. *I'm sorry I'm sorry I'm sorry Amalee, God, please believe me, I never meant it I shouldn't have said it I repent.*

And it doesn't even matter for me, not really, because I can kneel in church every day forever and search for answers, but it's Amalee, Amalee whose soul is damned, and maybe she wouldn't be damned, wouldn't have killed herself, would have made it through the nightmares if I had only kept my mouth shut and it's not her fault, not her fault at all, and God, please God, forget about *me*, just save my sister. Save my big sister, please, God, save her so I don't have to do this terrible thing.

And a voice like no other whispers **Forgiven** in my ear, and the sex feeling explodes in me again, rolling on and on and on, forever and ever and ever.

Amalee rises up from within her own dead body, a bright and brilliant soul full of laughter, the way she was before the nightmares began.

You have a gift now, she whispers, *a gift the Nightmares will always try to take. You might not live long, sweetheart, but none of us do, in the Mad City. Best you can do is live well, baby sister. Hold on to the light. Save who you can and don't give in to the power over death. Don't wreck your soul.*

My sister fades away, and the Devil's handsome face cracks with rage. The Nightmares burst through, tearing and shredding at my skin, but just now, right now, in this moment, they can't touch me.

In this moment, I am become Death, but not destroyer of worlds. I am light, I am loss, I am love. I lift my hands, still bright with Amalee's passing. My Nightmares shriek and run from that power. From the power of hope. And once they've run, the Devil's pretty face is back in place, and he falls back into step with me. He'll never leave me, but he'll never win.

Just as long as I don't rest my head.

CE MURPHY has held the usual grab-bag of jobs usually seen in an authorial biography, including public library volunteer, archival assistant, cannery worker, and web designer. Writing books is better, and she now has close to twenty in print. In her down time, she writes comic books and short stories, which may be why her editor and agent independently suggested she get a hobby that *wasn't* writing.

She was born and raised in Alaska, and now lives with her family in her ancestral homeland of Ireland.

DON'T SPILL YOUR TEA

BY JOSH ROBY

I FLING OUT A DESPERATE HAND, none too coordinated, and feel it make contact with something hard. Things clatter, fall to the ground. The lights jiggle around me, and I squeeze my eyes shut to make it stop. The blaring klaxons keep wailing, sending hot pokers into my temples. I flail again, and this time my fingers find purchase, groping blindly, until they reach their target. The alarm suddenly squelches silent, but I know it's only a short reprieve.

The snooze button only quiets my alarm clock for nine minutes.

Bleary-faced, I poke my head up over my pillow to see how many times I've already hit snooze. The red readout tries to hide behind the bottles of prescription sleep aids (as close to horse tranquilizers you can get while still being intended for human consumption), but my sleep-addled brain is still able to put the digits together. 6:57. With a mutter and groan, I swing my heavy arms under me and push. Time to get up.

Adelaide is of course already awake and waiting for me, sitting on the edge of her bed and playing tea party with Pooh Bear, Off-Brand Barbie, and Optimus Prime. Sometimes I worry about her toys giving her body image issues: when she grows up, will she be disappointed that she isn't a truck? But this early in the morning, I'm going on auto-pilot and with the lingering effects of the sleeping pills I mostly just register excited morning hugs and the need to make breakfast.

The next half-hour is mostly a blur that ends with me watching her board the school bus, lunch box in hand, and waving. I wave to her through the window and I wave to the woman holding on to the top of the bus, dressed in a trenchcoat and holding a katana in her hand. She gives me a short nod, and I turn to head back to the house. Everything is right with the world.

On the way, my phone buzzes in the pocket of my bathrobe and I fish it out. The calendar is telling me that the First Client of the Day is at 8am. Why are all the words capitalized, I think as I thumb open the appointment. But there are no details. Just First Client of the Day. And that's when I start to wonder what I do for a living.

There's a woman at my front door, rapping on the metal screen and making it rumble like tinny thunder. I cast a quick glance across the street, where a bum is leaning against a fence. He indicates her with a dip of his head and gives me a thumbs-up, which is somewhat reassuring.

I scuff my feet on the walk so my visitor hears me coming, and she whirls around, eyes crazy. "Are you Joe Fix?"

I scowl. "What?"

"Droop-Eyed Joe. Joe Fix," she insists. "I… I have an appointment?" She's somewhere in her 20s but she talks and moves like a teenager: all hurry and insistence. Asian, with close-cropped hair that she might have cut herself with kitchen scissors. Buttoned up in a battered old coat against the morning chill, but showing a black collar creeping up her throat and black leggings and boots beneath the hem.

I rub my face. "You must be my first client of the day."

She snaps her fingers. "That's what I was supposed to say."

"I do business over here," I say automatically, pointing around the house towards the garage. There's a side door over here, which opens into the laundry room, except when I open the door there's a desk and the walls are covered with paper-stuffed shelves. I stop in the doorway, hand still on the knob, and for the life of me the first question that comes to mind is how I'm going to get the day's laundry done.

A moment later, though, it all starts coming back, and I start to curse.

"What?" the woman asks, standing on tip-toe to look inside. "Is something wrong?"

"No, nothing's wrong," I say, stepping inside and gesturing her to-wards the chair on the client side of the desk. "I just remembered what I do for a living. I deal with you people."

"Us people?"

I drop myself into the other chair. "You people. How long since you've slept?"

She shrugs, but it's so sudden and violent it might be one big twitch. "I don't know. A few weeks?"

I nod, opening up a manila folder. It's the only one on the desk, set directly in the center as if waiting. Inside is a home-made form with blanks and spaces for notes. At the top is a trio of short paragraphs labeled, "Read This First." I frown, scan a line or two, and realize I'm supposed to read it out loud to her.

"So this is how this works," I read to her. "You're a Waker, I'm a Sleeper. I used to be a Waker, though, and I can get you things."

"I need—" she starts, but I hold up a hand.

"In return, I need some favors from you. First and foremost, I need protection from the things in… Mad City." I pause for a moment at that, but then it feels right. I continue on. "I'm sure you already met my friend across the street when you arrived today. One thing you can do for me is take a shift being my friend across the street. Or something else: I always have things that need doing. Is this your first time here?"

She bobs her head, and so I read her the If It's Their First Time paragraph: "For first-timers, I need payment up front. You tend not to come back. Once we establish a relationship, and I'm moderately sure you won't get yourself killed or eaten, you can owe me and I'll call you when I need you. Do you understand?"

She bobs her head again, and then sees that I'm done, so she says, "Yes. I understand. They told me you could get me what I need."

I fold my hands over the form. "What do you need?"

"I need some T-E-A," she says, spelling out the letters. I wait for her to explain. "That is… Triethylaluminum."

I nod, and a tickle of memory at the back of my brain suggests that I have had stranger-sounding requests. "And what is this… trietha… TEA?"

"It's an industrial compound used in… I'm a chemist," she says suddenly, switching tracks. "That is, I'm trained as one. I almost got my doctorate, and then…"

"And then the Mad City," I nod. "There was… some embarrassment at your school, I assume?"

"They think I'm crazy!" she spits suddenly. "Doctor Fattah had a parasite boring into her neck and everyone ignored it. I tried to help— I did help—but the only way to get it off was hydrochloric acid…"

I write "chemist" down in the space on the form labeled, "Other Skills," until she winds down. "What is TEA?" I ask again, with all the patience of a cat-herder.

"It's a catalyst, you use it to make plastics," she tells me as if this was obvious.

"And you're looking to make plastic?"

"No, no," she answers too quickly, then laughs. "No, I need it to end Mad City. I'm going to bring it all down, Joe. Should I call you Joe? There's a pillar, you see. The Wax King has it, in his castle. The pillar is his castle, really. Or at least it's the center of it. And it holds up everything. If it comes down, so does Mad City."

I maintain eye contact and nod as if I'm listening. This is why first-timers pay up front. If I got her this TEA, she'd go haring off to throw herself in front of the Wax King, and even with my fog-dimmed memory, I know she's not coming back. The King is powerful, dangerous, and jealous of his own power and position. Threatening the King is a one-way ticket to getting your face and soul melted off. And he has uses for half-melted, half-forgotten half-people. I shudder a little, and that brings her monologue to an end.

"Are you all right?"

I straighten the form and folder against the corners of the desk blotter. "I'm fine. Can you tell me what TEA is?"

"Didn't I already?" she blinks, frowns, then beams. "I suppose I didn't, did I? It will melt the pillar."

"Through some chemical reaction?"

Now she guffaws, eye glinting and lips stretched wide. Perfect teeth. She shakes her head and breathes deep to stop herself from laughing. "No, no, of course not. TEA ignites when exposed to air. You... you can't put it out."

I tick the boxes labeled Dangerous and Probably Illegal. "Let's shift gears, then. What can you do?"

By happy coincidence, she can walk through walls, and I have a message that needs delivering to somebody in the state penitentiary. She asks why, as first-timers often do, and I tell her that I don't ask questions. The answers I get rarely make much sense, anyway. "What's important," I tell her, "is that you deliver this message and I get you your TEA."

She stands and I see her to the door. Before she goes, she turns and gets a funny smile on her face. "You used to be like me. Like us people."

I bob my head. "I did. A few years ago my daughter went missing. I couldn't sleep for worry, and after a few days I started to see things. Hallucinations, at least that's what they all seem to be at first, but the things they did and said started to make too much sense when you put them all together. Long story short, they'd taken my daughter to Mad City. I had to go fetch her."

"They say you're the one who put the crater in the Bazaar."

"I figured they would have paved over it by now."

She shakes her head. "No, they just built new stalls on top of it. But the ground dips like crazy there." She squeezes the scrap of paper I'd given her in her hand, then licks her lips. "Listen, I'm going to go do this now, but… tonight when my friends and I hit the Wax Castle, we could use your help."

I put a hand on the door, hoping she'll take the hint and leave. "I don't do that anymore."

"Joe, it's the last battle," she says, not taking the hint. "I mean, this is it. This is the end. Don't you want to be there?"

"I want to be home when my daughter is home," I tell her simply. "If I'm not, there wasn't much sense in me going to get her in the first place, was there?" I don't say, I'd rather scrape out a life with Adelaide than be a whacked-out nutjob fighting a holy war against bad guys who are probably more than half imaginary. A bit of that emotion creeps into what I do say, though, and a cloud crosses her face. She waves the scrap of paper, gives me a short nod, and leaves.

My next client is already waiting outside.

He needs a "doctor's note" to get extended leave from his job while he "solves" his current crop of problems. I'm not a doctor, but I have some believable stationary that says I am. The next one needs money delivered to her family; I don't ask where the money comes from. I conduct another client into my showroom, the garage, in which I have two display racks that fold down from the ceiling. They're full of guns, but it's actually a rare Waker who comes to me for a gun. And those that do are rarely repeat customers. The Mad City doesn't respond well to the obvious, and it angers easily. More come and go, and I log all their needs and their potential services in my files.

A little after lunch, Nyx comes by bearing gifts. Nyx isn't a Waker, but he does know about the Mad City—mostly because he's from there. I met him when I rescued Adelaide. He was, in fact, rather helpful. Back then, he was a dissatisfied minion of the monster that took Adelaide: a big brute on a demonic horse with a factory full of little girls… I don't like to think about it for obvious reasons. Anyway, with the Horseman gone, Nyx moved up the ladder and took control of the factory himself. No more child labor—and no more manufacturing little girls, either. Everybody came out a winner.

These days, Nyx has a habit of arriving at my door with very good Scotch and we talk shop. Admittedly, I'm never very good at remembering the details once I hit the pillow, but I enjoy our talks, if only because it's nice to deal with somebody who doesn't need something from me. In my line of work, it's a rare thing to win respect from somebody who doesn't have cause to be grateful at the same time.

This time, he's bitching about the cost of doing business in the Bazaar. The widgets he makes are undervalued because of the recent influx by lucid dreams of similar widgets. "And of course I can't prove anything, old man, but it seems deliberate to me," he says, and absently smoothes the line of his slate grey suit jacket. "Somebody out there is getting people to daydream about my widgets, and then using those dreams to undercut my bottom line."

"Can you diversify?" I ask, hoping this sounds like a reasonable response. I'm no businessman, so I have to masquerade as one to keep up my end of the conversation. Of course, Nyx isn't a businessman either, just a nightmare about businessmen, and so my faking it doesn't usually matter.

"Widgets are widgets," he shrugs, waving his tumbler lazily. "They used to be precision goods, but with recent advances in production, they're really just commodities, at this point. Interchangeable." He shrugs again, this time more 'could be worse' than 'it doesn't matter.' "Same thing is happening to a lot of markets. Tears, pig iron, personality quirks, fiber optic cable, tea…"

"Tea leaves and not TEA," I put in with a smirk, happy to have an iota of interesting data to contribute to the conversation.

"Triethylaluminum?" he asks immediately, and my hopes of explaining what it is and sounding authoritative dissipate.

"Not exactly a commodity, is it?" I try, forcing a slight smile.

"Hard to come by," he nods his head. "That's why the plant abandoned plastics and shifted production to a moral indignation supply pipeline." A slow smile creeps across his pencil-thin lips. "Industrial chemicals fall a little outside your bailiwick, old man. What brings TEA bubbling up to the surface of your mind, today?"

I shrug. "A client came looking for it. Out here in the Slumber, it's easy enough to get hold of some with the proper papers." I allow myself a triumphant smile. "According to the documents another client forged for me a while back, I've been a licensed manufacturer of handheld electronics for fifteen years."

"Factory floor out in the backyard?" Nyx asks with a conspiratorial grin. We share a chuckle and sip Scotch. A few moments later, he asks, "What's one of your clients want with TEA? The Awake are not, as a rule, known for making things."

I wave my own tumbler. "Your typical save-the-world scheme. Wants to burn down some pillar in the Wax King's castle."

"Oh, so somebody from your side finally found the pillar, eh?" Nyx asks, nodding to himself.

I raise an eyebrow, feigning nonchalance. "I never know if what my clients tell me is real or imaginary... or if they're fixating on some crazy unimportant detail as if it's the meaning of existence."

"Oh, the axis mundi is real."

I settle back into my chair and eye the clock. I have another appointment soon, and will have to make my excuses. "What's it do?"

"It holds up everything," he shrugs, and polishes off his drink. He considers what's left in his glass. "Her crazy scheme might work, actually," he allows, and then chuckles. "If she could get into the castle, but it's... well, it's a fortress, isn't it? Getting past all those knights, dealing with the gates and walls... it'd take an army. And I don't think you're selling armies as well as obscure chemicals, eh?"

He surges up to his feet and I follow suit. He nods at the clock and I give him the tight, apologetic smile of two peers who understand that our time is up without needing to resort to words. I almost mention, by way of conversation, that the client in question can walk through walls, but he talks and I listen as he heads for my front door.

"Tell me something, Joe. Why is that the Awake always assume that theirs is the real world, and our city is some sort of fake shadow?" He finds his coat, hat, and scarf on the pegs by the door and dons them. "Who says that the City Slumbering isn't just the tip of the iceberg, and our world is what's really real, down under the surface?"

Metaphysics is one of Nyx' favorites, and one of my weaker subjects. I just shrug. "Bias, I guess. Your hometown is always what's normal and honest and good. It's other people from other places that you've got to worry about."

Nyx nods with approval. "I suppose you're right, for most people." He thrusts forward his hand for a goodbye shake. "I'm glad some of us are able to rise above such small-minded assumptions."

I shake vigorously and smile. "Me, too, Nyx. See you sometime next week?"

"Absolutely." He tips his hat and steps out into the balmy afternoon. I watch him go until he passes behind a tree and doesn't come out the other side.

The next client needs bolt cutters, which sounds pretty prosaic until he tells me he needs two hundred of them and they have to be a certain model from a certain manufacturer. I have a wholesaler's license, too, so that isn't much of a problem, especially since he's also a reliably successful bank robber. He leaves two duffel bags of cash with me and I tell him the bolt cutters will be here in a couple days. Then it's time to go pick up Adelaide at the bus stop.

The afternoon passes in a blur, as most afternoons do. I juggle seeing Adelaide home, feeding her a healthy snack, and prodding her into doing some homework while at the same time I am arranging for a garbage pickup across town (inside the fridge is either a body or a pile of push-pins, or both), ordering hardware in bulk, and receiving a 60-gallon drum full of a volatile chemical. I don't generally take appointments once Adelaide is home—sleepless crazy is contagious, sometimes—so mostly I do phone-errands until dinner and a TV show and bedtime.

The chemist returns long after the night has gone full dark. The hollows under her eyes seem deeper in the neon lighting inside my garage, but her frenetic energy bubbles over when she sees the drum and its OSHA warning label. She has a shopping bag from Beer&More, and from it she produces a tangle of aluminum pipes and hoses.

"I haven't seen one of those since the keggers of my college years," I say, and eye the thick metal drum skeptically. "Will that work?"

"I've got a friend who can make it work," she says, and sets the party pump on top of the drum. It makes a deep bwong, sounding very heavy. She looks to the hand truck sitting against the wall. "I didn't think about moving it once I had it…"

I expected this, so I slide the hand truck under the drum and tip it back onto the wheels. "I happened to be making a hardware order today and I already got myself a replacement. This one's yours."

"That's very thoughtful of you," she says, looking me up and down. Here comes the gratitude.

"We're a full-service operation here," I say for lack of anything better.

"Have you thought any more about coming along?" she asks, still staring at me. Her hips cant to the side and she smiles. This is the hard sell. Her sagging eyes and her ragged hair ruin any allure she might have been capable of directing my way. She doesn't look bold or daring or exciting. She looks like a crazy person with a drum of toxic chemicals.

"I don't do that anymore," I tell her again.

"But Joe, we're going to bring it all down," she insists, stepping towards me. She gestures behind her at the TEA. "I can wheel this right into the middle of the Wax Castle and spray it all over the pillar. Fwoom. That pillar is the only thing holding the Mad City apart from the real world, Joe. When it melts, the two worlds will be reunited. No more nightmares. No more insomnia-powered hijinks."

It's a moment before I shake my head, but it's not hesitation like she thinks. She waves her hands at the garage and the minivan. "No more living in this fortified outpost in suburbia, Joe, no more having to deal with Us People and our crazy requests. It'll all be over. Everything will go back to normal."

"Will it? And you know this how?"

"Because it's not natural," she tells me. "The place where you sleep and the place where dreams live... they shouldn't be different places. You don't... you don't go anywhere when you sleep, or at least you shouldn't. You should stay where you are and your dreams should be your own, not hitched up to some crazy Jungian train wreck."

"Us living our lives, sleeping and dreaming," I lead her along. "That's what's natural. That's what's... really real, right? Or should be."

"Exactly!" she grins a mile wide.

"Who told you that melting the axis mundi would end the Mad City?"

The grin falters. "The what?"

"The axis… the wax pillar inside the castle."

She shakes her head. "The King himself told us that it kept the worlds separate. We worked out the rest ourselves."

"So you don't know," I insist. "You don't know for certain what happens. You don't even have a good guess. You have a hope."

"Hope's enough," she tells me fiercely. "Hope's all I've got left, Joe. And whatever happens, it's got to be better than the way things are now."

I look past her, to the parked minivan, to the sun-faded outdoor toys stashed up on a shelf, to the trampoline in the corner. "I like the way things are now," I hear myself say.

"What?"

"Did it ever occur to you," I ask, "that maybe instead of destroying the Mad City you'd just drop our world into that… mess? Maybe our world isn't the real world. Maybe our world only exists because it's not drowning in the Mad City."

"That's just crazy," she says, and I laugh at that coming out of her. She doesn't take this as a good sign, though, and hefts the hand truck backwards as if to go. "Listen, thanks for this stuff. Once everything is over, I'll come back and we can laugh about—"

By that point I've crossed the garage and pulled down the display rack. I grab the handgun at the top, the one I keep loaded and fixed with a silencer, and swing it around to bear on her. Her eyes go wide and she yanks the hand truck hard, wheeling it towards the closed garage door. Her right hand swings forward for balance, and when it reaches the aluminum door it passes right through. Her whole body strains to follow.

I squeeze off three shots, but at this range the last two aren't necessary. The inside of my garage door gets painted sudden crimson. Her right arm falls back to her side minus a hand, and then she crumples to the floor. The drum totters on the wheels of the hand truck, then falls forward. The seal around the edge of the drum breaks, and out pours what looks like water, but the air is suddenly redolent with chemical reek. A moment later the TEA bursts into flame, and I dash for the garage's side door.

I cross over to the house, pull open the door to the laundry room, and grab the phone. I push one of the auto-dial numbers and step back outside. The garage is lighting up quickly, the door already a sheet of flame. A pool of TEA seeps out onto the driveway beyond, followed by wheeling fire. The puddle finds its way to the severed hand sitting on the driveway. A moment later it's blistered and blackened and then it's barely recognizable... much like the garage.

Somebody on the other end of the line picks up. "Joe?"

"Hey Sam," I say, wincing at the heat and retreating into the laundry room. "I've got a little problem over at my house. I need a crime scene covered up."

The voice sniffs. "And then you and I are clear?"

"Oh hell yes," I nod, even though Sam can't see it. "Somebody's going to call 911 in a minute—there's a fire—so the first responders will be here real soon."

"I'll be there first," comes the response, followed by a click.

I return the phone to its charging cradle in the laundry room, then make my way through the house to Adelaide's room. I crack open the door slowly and quietly, then creep inside to her bedside. Her breathing is even and shallow, and she twitches just slightly. Dreams. I bend over and brush a light kiss on her temple, then beat my silent retreat.

In my room, I shuck out of my clothes and grab a handful of sleep aids. I munch them down and crawl into bed.

Tomorrow's a big day.

JOSH ROBY is a little-more-than thirty-year-old writer, editor, and layout artist, scraping his way to fame and fortune, or hopefully at least a decent living. You can find his stuff or even hire him at *joshroby.com.*

DON'T FORGET YOUR KIDS

BY MATT FORBECK

Loman was so tired he couldn't remember his first name. He only knew that he had to get home in time to get his kids back to his ex. If he wasn't there right when she showed up, she'd keep on going, and he'd be stuck with them for another two weeks at least.

He couldn't recall how many times in a row this had already happened, but he felt sure he'd broken all records, and he needed a break. Abby and Ben had soared so far past getting on each other's nerves they'd cut straight to the bone. Like most nights, he'd stormed out of the house after screaming at them to just shut up, and he'd headed down to the bar for a drink.

Ben was a handful, he knew, but Abby was plenty old enough to take care of him, no matter how much she bitched about it or how often he had to break up their fights. Sometimes he thought they did better together when he wasn't there. It removed some fucked up part of their family dynamic that he didn't really understand but that his ex liked to go on about every chance she got.

Or maybe he was just kidding himself, rationalizing away his need for some time to himself.

He was a good dad, or at least he did the best that he could. He loved his kids. But the way his marriage had gone, he knew that love wasn't always enough.

Loman signaled the bartender for another shot. The fat-faced man in a too-tight polo with the "Quitting Time" logo stitched over his left breast brought over a bottle of Laphroaig and topped off Loman's glass.

"Bit richer than your usual," the bartender said.

Loman pulled a wad of cash from his pocket, peeled off a twenty, and slid it onto the bar. "Guess I'm flush today."

"Find your son yet?"

"What?" Loman stared at the bartender.

"Your son. He was missing, right?"

Loman swallowed hard and rubbed his eyes. "Right." He glanced into the mirror behind the bar. He looked like walking death, circles under his eyes so black they'd gone to forest green while his eyes were shot through with red.

He glanced at the clock that hung at one end of the bar, the numbers hanging below the shimmering river of a old Hamm's sign. Its glowing red digits read 13:15.

"I gotta go." Loman pushed himself away from the bar and staggered toward the exit.

"What about your change?" the barkeeper called after him.

"Keep it."

It wasn't like Loman to toss money around like that, but nothing was more important than his boy—except getting drunk on fine Scotch, it seemed. What the hell had he been thinking?

Ben had been gone for how long now? Two weeks? Four? It seemed like Loman had been searching for him forever. He'd only gone into the bar to take a break. He deserved it. Hell, he needed it.

But break time was over.

Loman stumbled into the streets and stared up at the muddy, starless sky. He needed to get out of here, to put this damned city behind him, maybe take the kids out camping somewhere in the woods, someplace open and free, with clean air and a canopy of sparkling lights overhead. He just needed to find Ben first.

He thought about calling home. Maybe Ben had come back while he was out and Abby was taking care of him right now, tucking him in for the night.

Of course, if that was true, she'd have called.

Instead, Loman steeled himself for another long night of wandering the empty streets, hoping to find some sign of Ben. The police wouldn't help him, he knew. He'd tried them already, and those goddamn clock-punchers had already given up on the boy.

Thankfully Loman's ex hadn't gotten wind of it yet. Once she did, she'd scream for his head. He'd lose Abby then, too.

Part of Loman wished for that. He'd gone to the papers to ask them for help looking for Ben, but they'd ignored him. He knew they thought he was crazy, but when a boy went missing, wasn't that news?

So it was Loman against the world again. Alone. Some other part of him suspected that was the way he liked it.

Most of the city seemed to be asleep at this time of night. Loman wanted to sleep, to let the soft fingers of night take him away, cover him and heal him, and present him fresh and new to a shiny sunlit day. He wanted it more than just about anything, but not more than he wanted his son.

Loman heard the commotion coming before he saw it, a sharp roar of voices rising and falling in an unintelligible cacophony. When he turned the corner, stepping over a homeless man whose legs had sprawled into the sidewalk, he spotted the source of the sound down a long alley that led through an ordered darkness and emerged into a bright-lit chaos.

Loman knew better than to walk down a dark alley in any city, much less this one, but the noise and the fervor it carried with it hooked him and reeled him in. He wondered if the same thing had happened to Ben. The boy was so much like him—too much, his ex often said.

Loman picked his way past the piles of garbage and the piss-splashed walls, glancing in every direction as he moved, his senses jagged as a junkie's knife as he scanned the darkness for threats both real and imagined. Nothing happened. No one came at him. Not a drug dealer or a prostitute or a bum. Especially not Ben.

As the alley opened up again, Loman found himself standing on the edge of a massive open-air market the size of a full city block. People of all sorts crowded through it, picking their way through the crowded tables, open-topped stalls, and roof-only tents. Merchandise of all kinds mounded up everywhere, threatening to topple over at the lightest touch, and voices rose and fell as buyers asked questions about quality and sellers haggled over price.

"Ben?" The word sprang from a throat now parched, and Loman wished he'd bought the bottle of Scotch to take with him. He tried again, louder. "Ben!"

A few heads turned toward him, but most just continued on with their business. One young man with long hair and a brown goatee turned toward him with a gleeful grin and shouted, "Sure, I have, man! Who hasn't?"

Then he turned and strode off laughing at some joke that Loman couldn't understand.

Loman ignored him and plunged into the bazaar instead, hunting for his son. He couldn't remember ever having been in a place like this before, but it still seemed familiar, like he'd been drunk or drugged when he'd been dragged through it once. He felt like he knew what he'd find around every corner, even though he couldn't seem to see it first.

He stalked through the aisles, past stalls that sold strange foods, butchers hawking haunches cut from animals he'd never known. Eyeballs turned up toward him from within steaming pots of soup, and he could swear they watched him as he passed by. One tent that seemed to be made of glittering scales sold man-sized sets of wings the horse-faced owner claimed would "do you better than a case of Red Bull." Another, under a wide banner that read "Prima Facie," offered the most lifelike masks Loman had ever seen.

"Looking for a trade-in, mister?" the sultry woman behind the stall's front table asked as he walked by. "Not sure what I can give you for a face you've mistreated so, but I can upgrade you to one of our latest models for a song."

"What?" Loman turned toward her. She had the features of a supermodel, although her eyes danced with the wisdom few of those young ladies ever seemed to have.

"That's all. Just your favorite song." The woman winked at him. "I know. Seems like a real steal, don't it?"

"I'm looking for my son," Loman said.

"Out here?" The woman's eyes flew wide. "Good luck. This ain't no place for a kid."

"Don't you think I know that?" Loman clenched his fists before him. He wanted to break something, anything, but he worried about what it might cost him in a place like this.

The woman put up her hands to placate him. "Hey, I'm the last person who should be giving out parenting advice. Just ask my kids."

"I don't care about your kids," Loman said. "I just want my son back."

The woman's smile froze on her face, and Loman wondered if he'd gone too far. He didn't much care right then though.

Someone bumped into him then, hard, and Loman spun around to give the bastard a piece of his mind. "Hey, asshole!"

As the words left his mouth, Loman regretted them. He stopped with his mouth wide open as he stared at the man's blue-jacketed back and spotted a large brass key jutting out from it, the kind that Loman had used to wind up toys as a kid except as big around as a hubcap. The policeman it was attached to turned about on hinky legs and stared back at Loman with eyes somehow both glassy and suspicious, as if they'd been painted on him that way.

"What seems to be the problem, citizen?" The officer wore a wide, plastic grin that did not move as he spoke.

"Nothing." Loman backed into the stall filled with faces. "Nothing at all."

"Surely there's something wrong?" the officer said. "Doesn't everyone have a problem? We are only here to help."

The woman in the booth reached out and put a possessive hand on Loman's shoulder. "Nothing we can't solve on our own, sir," she said.

"Everyone can use a little help." The officer stepped closer, his movements jerky and somehow still precise.

"Is it the custom of Officer Tock's men to interfere with the business of the Bizarre Bazaar?" the woman said. "And now, during the busiest hour of our day?"

The officer stopped cold. Perhaps his face would have flinched if it could have moved. "Of course not," the officer said. "Carry on, citizens."

Loman watched the officer spin on a heel and then march away. The giant key in his back ratcheted clockwise with every step he took.

The woman patted Loman on the back, and he turned around to give her a sheepish look. "I'm sorry," he said. "I'm upset about my boy."

"You're missing Ben," she said. "Do you have a picture of him?" She gestured to the merchandise dangling from her walls. "I never forget a face."

Loman fished out his wallet and opened it to Ben's latest school photo. He'd not been able to afford to pay for school pictures this year, but they'd sent one home anyhow, framed on a card he was supposed to be able to give the authorities if his kid turned up missing. Not that it had done him any good.

The woman stared at the picture and pursed her too-perfect lips together into a pair of cupid bows. She handed it back to him with a sad, tired look in her eyes. "You need to go see the Fortune Taker."

Loman narrowed his eyes in confusion, and she sighed. She bent over the table and pointed off to the left, deeper into the bazaar. "Thirteen stalls down and six rows to the right."

"Thank you." Loman took the woman's hand and shook it with gratitude. This was the first lead he'd had in longer than he could remember. "Who should I say sent me?"

"You can call me Prima." She gave him a tender smile. "All my friends do."

Loman nodded his thanks and then set off into the bazaar once more. He followed Prima's directions to the letter and soon found himself standing in front of a stall curtained on all four sides with blue velvet. The sign out front of it read "Fortunes Bought and Sold."

The curtains on the front of the stall opened, and a burly woman dressed in a janitor's overalls and a black silk top hat stepped out from between them. "Can I help you?" she said.

Her voice caught in her throat as she spotted Loman standing in the aisle before her, and she grimaced and put out a hand for him. "Of course. Of course I can."

Loman let her take him by the hand and lead him inside the tent. It had seemed large enough on the outside, but the inside seemed far smaller, as tight as a womb. There was only room for two cafe chairs and a small round table between them.

A light glowed from the table's surface, and as the woman sat down in the farther chair, the shadows it cast gave her face a sinister aspect. Unbidden, Loman sat down in the chair opposite the woman and her well-worn face and wondered if he looked the same way to her. She gave him a nervous smile before she spoke.

"And how can I help you today, Mr. Loman?"

Loman flinched at the thought that the woman knew him. Perhaps Prima had phoned ahead, but had he given her his name either? He couldn't recall.

"I've lost my son," Loman said.

The woman reached out and gave his hand a gentle pat with her wrinkled fingers. "I know."

"I want—" Loman hesitated. What did he want? Did he even know any more. "Can you help me find him?"

"Yes." The woman leaned forward, inquisitive and earnest. "Are you sure that's what you want?"

"More than anything." Tears came to his eyes, but he blinked them back. "Please. Help me."

The woman sighed. "I thought I already had."

Loman narrowed his eyes at the woman. "Have we met?"

"You sold me something." She shook her head at him. "Don't you remember?"

Loman shuddered and shook his head right back at her. "Miss?"

"Call me Lethe." She folded her hands on the table before her. "You don't know what you're asking."

Loman frowned, but he reached across the table to take her hands and reassure her. "I don't think I know much of anything anymore. All I know for sure is that I have to find my little boy. I have to find my Ben."

"All right." Lethe made a face as if a bug had flown into her mouth. "There's the matter of payment."

Loman reached into his pocket and yanked out his wad of cash. "You can have it. All of it."

Lethe shook her head. "I'm afraid it doesn't work that way. I can give the memory of your son back to you, but you must give me another in return. Something happy."

Loman stared at the woman. "Are you insane?"

Lethe leaned back and folded her arms across her chest. "I don't recommend you do this. It will not give you what you want."

Loman shoulders slumped. "All I want to know is what happened to my boy."

Lethe gave him a reluctant nod. "All right," she said, steel in her voice. "Remember this if nothing else: you insisted."

Loman nodded, putting out his hands for her again. She put hers in his, and he held them like a lifeline.

"And what will you pay?"

Loman swallowed. He tried to remember the happiest times in his life, and one sprang to mind in an instant. "My wedding day."

The memory of that day had soured along with his relationship with his wife, but he found that he still treasured it. He brought it with him to bed at night and wallowed in it sometimes, picking at it like a scab that would never heal. As much as he loved it, he knew he'd be better off without it.

"So be it," Lethe said. She closed her eyes, and Loman did the same.

"Think of your memory," Lethe said, "for the last time."

Loman did as she asked. He remembered standing at the altar, in front of his family and friends, and watching his ex stride up the center aisle toward him, her feet sliding along the white runner. He pictured the flowers she'd had woven into her hair, and the blush on her cheeks as he'd raised her veil. He'd never know her or anyone else to be more beautiful than she was to him in that particular moment. He looked into her eyes and knew that he loved her, and she loved him, and that it would last forever.

And then it was gone, disappeared like it had never been. Try as he might, Loman could not conjure up his ex's face any longer, not from that day at least. All he could remember now was the way it had all gone bad, the hatred that shone in her eyes now when she looked at him, glittering right there alongside all the pain he'd caused her.

Loman bowed his head to weep, the tears flowing from his eyes as if he'd sprung twin leaks. Then the memories that he'd asked for came flooding back into him, and he shoved himself back away from the table and screamed.

He remembered it, every damn second, and he wanted it gone.

He'd come home late that night, drunk again, and he'd found Abby waiting for him, sobbing at the bottom of the stairs. He'd gone to her, stretching out a hand to comfort her, to ask what was wrong. That's when he'd seen Ben lying in her arms, blanched and still.

Abby had looked up at him, her face swollen and twisted in grief. "I didn't mean it, Daddy," she'd said. "We were fighting on the stairs. He called me—he called me a bitch, and I—I slapped him."

Loman had looked down in horror to see his son's head sitting on his shoulders at an impossible angle.

"He fell, Daddy. He fell down the stairs. I didn't mean it."

Loman shoved the memories away. He couldn't take them anymore. They made him want to claw his eyes from his face, and he found his fingers already digging into his lids.

"I told you," Lethe said. She had stood and backed away from him. "I warned you."

Loman glared at the woman in horror and fury. She'd taken off her top hat now and held it before her like a shield, as if that could have stopped him. He had never hated anyone so much in his life right then, with one exception.

"How much?" he said with a growl that made Lethe flinch.

"What do you mean?"

Loman pounded the table between them so hard that the glowing surface cracked. The flight flickered and threatened to go out.

"You buy memories." Loman jabbed a finger into his temple. "How much? How much for them all?"

Lethe cleared her throat and put her silk hat back on top of her head. She sat down at the table and looked up at him, cold and businesslike again. "I'm sure we can make a deal."

MATT FORBECK has been a full-time creator of award-winning games and fiction since 1989. He has designed games and toys and written stories of all sorts. He has sixteen novels published to date, including the award-nominated *Guild Wars: Ghosts of Ascalon* and the critically acclaimed *Amortals* and *Vegas Knights.* His latest work includes the *Magic: The Gathering* comic book and the historical horror novel *Carpathia.* He is currently in the middle of his 12 for '12 project, in which he's writing a novel every month this year. For more about him and his work, visit *Forbeck.com*.

DON'T TOOT YOUR HORN

BY LAURA ANNE GILMAN

UNLIKE THE SAX, THE TROMBONE BLASTS ITS WAY onto the scene, sliding like a triumphant runner into third base, giving the rest of the band a neener-neener as it brushes itself off and accepts the accolades of the crowd. You needed a certain kind of arrogance to pick up a trombone, and you needed even more to keep playing until you got the hang of it.

Dax had been playing since he was eleven, his battered second-hand horn squeaking and slipping until it finally bowed to his will. He'd worked so many nightclubs and offsite shows, he'd forgotten more than he'd ever remember, one gig sliding until another until he couldn't remember sleeping, either.

He'd done all the classics: booze, sex, pills, then shooting it straight into his veins, but it hadn't been until he wandered down the wrong alley one night, half out of his mind with exhaustion and speed, that he'd figured it out.

Mad City.

Now, it was all he could remember. Him, and the horn, and the bitch-goddess of the tune, walking that razor balance.

Thirteenth hour was coming; the Bazaar was getting too thick, shadow-eyed Wakies crowding in alongside locals, poking into stands and fingering wares, clotted and cloudy and hot to deal. Dax slung his horn over his shoulder and headed for elsewhere.

"You."

Since the figure was standing in front of him, looking at him with dead eyes, Dax didn't bother trying to ignore or avoid it.

"Me."

"You're wanted."

Suddenly there was space around him, where you'd sworn there wasn't any to be found. Nobody wanted to be summoned, in Mad City, and nobody wanted to be near anyone who'd been summoned.

"This official?" He didn't recognize the golem in front of him; it wasn't a Clockwork, so he wasn't being hauled in under warrant, and Dax didn't have anything the Tacks Man would go after.

"You resisting?" The golem opened its mouth and showed a dark chasm within, the suggestion of infinite width and depth that could swallow a man whole.

"Nowhere else to go," he shrugged, which was truth enough. If he wasn't chasing down the thin line, he wasn't doing anything at all.

They didn't go to the District, and they didn't go underground. That should have eased a worry, except the golem led him up.

Dax looked at the ladder, and balked. "I don't do roofs."

"You do now."

The golem lifted a hand as though to indicate 'you first,' and thick grey claws curled over the edges of its fingers, wickedly sharp.

Dax went up. The handrails were wet, not the clean damp of rain, but something slick and sticky.

Like blood. Or something worse.

Dax didn't go to the Bazaar when most other folk did, when things got hectic, after thirteen o'clock. Too crowded then, with all the buyers and the sellers shouting out their deals, no room left in the air for music to breathe. But the before and the after, when folk and not-folk lingered around the edges, waiting and hoping, scraping by… that was the time for someone like him.

He'd been there that morning, what passed for dawn when you never saw the sun, just looming brick wreathed in gloom. His horn smooth in his hands, the bitter coffee sour in his gut, waiting for the moment to come, tap tapping on his bones.

"Once more, dear friends…" he muttered, resting his aching shoulders against the wall and limbering up his fingers. The wall seemed to shift and mutter against his bones, but Dax didn't pay that no mind no more. Things happened here. Especially here.

"Play us a song, Daxman. Play us a song."

The usual whisper, opening his session. They had their requests, all the shadows drifting past, the lost souls and the haunted ones. Locals mostly, folk who'd wandered here and gotten stuck, most of the life faded from them. For a while, they'd listen to him play, and something like color would return to their existence.

Even the paperboys—frantic little bastards that they were—paused when he put music in the air.

But Dax had his rules, and first and foremost was you pay before he'd play.

Ready now, he took off his cap, worn and patched, and put it on the ground. No sign, no patter, no need. They knew who he was.

The first came up out of the drifting crowd, crawling where its knees once had been. Tacks Man had been at this one. Dax blew a low and soulful note, and the local shivered as though in pain.

"You got nothing to offer me."

"I do."

Locals, mostly, were useless. But this one held out one hand, un-folded skeletal-thin fingers, and displayed its prize in its palm. Wafer thin, translucent blue, it would disappear if you looked too hard at it. Dax averted his gaze, watching sideways, and blew another note, so low, drawn from deep down in the quiet still sadness of the soul.

The blue fluttered, wings lifting, the glistening dampness evapo-rating, scenting the dry, dusty air with the faintest hint of something bitter and clean.

Dax blew another note, lighter and sweeter, and the blue flexed its wings, lifted off the wretched thing's palm, and flew towards him, dizzy and darting.

The first true notes of the song emerged, and the blue scrap—drawn as though by honey, slid into the battered, tarnished bell of the trombone, and disappeared.

Dax felt it slide into him, and on the next exhale, he heard it, smooth and sweet. First love, ages before, the last scrap of anything the poor wretch had saved. His now.

And music poured out, filling the alley, drawing the crowd nearer, vendors emerging from their stalls, halting mid-haggle; even the awful shadow of a nightmare, distracted from its tormenting. Dax didn't notice any of them.

The night before, he'd holed up in a café where the lights were low and the coffee black and bitter-strong. He shut out the noise and clatter around him, and polished his horn, as though a cloth and gloss could rid it of the nicks and tarnish of a decade's hard use.

Most left him be. Most, but not all.

"You're a nightmare yourself."

Dax didn't stop polishing, didn't look up. "You kiss your momma with that mouth?"

"No, but I ate yours."

Jingleman carried his piece with him, a matte black clarinet, but the reed was splintered, and Dax had never heard him play. It took some folk like that: there was too much here, for them. They listened too hard to the doubts that crawled in, drowned everything they had in the fear, kept their instruments with 'em like they might be the key out of Mad City, out of the mad night, the mad haze, the mad sharp stillness of the streets, back to what was real.

Dax didn't care about out. Real didn't matter to him no more. The more they paid, the more he played, the closer he got to The Moment. The note in the music that said, "You here, boy. You arrived."

"You got a point?" he asked now.

"I been watching you. Everyone has."

Everyone could mean no one. Or it could mean everyone. There were always eyes on you, in Mad City. Some were even still human.

"You take the last things they got left," Jingleman said, hugging his coat around him like it was cold. "You take the only things that hold 'em together."

"I don't take nothing. They give. They pay me to play the music, and they go away no worse off than before."

"Pay." Jingleman snorted. "Feed, more like."

Dax held his horn out to Jingleman. "You wanna try it?"

The other turned ashy-pale and scampered back, clutching his clarinet.

"Yeah. Thought not."

"Nightmare," Jingleman muttered, and fled into the shadows.

The café sometimes let him doss down, off-hours. Most nights, he walked the street. The need for sleep was an ever-lingering hunger, but starvation got familiar, else you wouldn't have gotten to the City anyway. That's what they all were, sleepless walkers, only some eyes were sleep-stuck closed, and others stuck open.

"Watch yourself! Comin' through!" A pack of newsboys, elbows tucked, heads down, skating through the streets like the hounds of hell on little boys' feet. Dax moved, same as everyone else, knocking into a washerwoman with eyes empty as burnt-out coal who hissed like a cat, pulling away.

"Little bastards," he muttered, but kept it in his mouth. Dax had no friends here, and newsboys were quick to take offense. He tugged his jacket closer, hitched his pants, and walked on.

Not every day brought him closer. Sometimes there wasn't nobody in the Bazaar needed to escape, even for a bit, or the things they offered didn't interest him none. Then he played for free, letting the notes screech and scamper like those newsboys on a tear, hot flash fading to slow cool, coaxing sounds he hadn't known existed out of the battered metal, setting them free and returning for more.

His own memories were a melancholy wail, shiver-quick and tattered, stutter-stop and jagged.

His first day here, the wax almost got him. Disorientated and not sure where'n hell he was, he'd bunked down in the tunnels, thinking they'd be safer, and woke with his left leg smothered. He didn't know about the King Underneath, then. Hadn't known to be wary of anything too smooth. He scraped most off, but the leg was never the same. He'd gotten street-side somehow, memory blurred, knees shaking. He'd drawn breath and looked around, looked hard then, and seen what was what.

This place didn't just eat its young, it ate everyone. It took whatever you got. The locals here, they were scraps, tattered remnants of whatever they'd been, all of them. Nightmares ruled, insanity made sense. Mad City ate you up, bite by bite.

Not him. He bit back.

The same thing that'd driven him here, saved him. Jazz lived in these streets, in the alleys and the weird-slicked rooftops, the swagger-sweet smell of the air like a thousand nightclubs , the guilt and the horror and the despair improvising around the single core of hope. Survive another day, find the way home, keep the fires burning. He ate that up, one dream, one memory at a time, wallowing in it, his e-ticket riding the heated edge of insomnia between madness and genius.

Bite back. Eat up. Never sleep. Every night, every note, might be the one.

That was the secret. You could go dog-mad, or give over to the nightmares, make a mistake and be dragged down and smothered, or torn to shreds, or simply fade away. Or you could embrace the hell, dig deep into it.

Dax—exhausted, aching, confused—staggered into the Bazaar pure by chance, the coldcast dawn after that first endless night. Found a bit of wall and put his back against it, and did the only thing he knew how. He played his soul into his horn, and what came out was like nothing he'd ever played before. Every ache, every moan, every delight he'd ever felt, every secret he'd ever kept or told, every burst of jism or bitter tear, raged out of his lungs and into the dry, dirty air. Ragged scales and wild flights, no notes ever marked on a staff, neither ending nor beginning but looping endlessly into itself, until he'd fallen forward, gasping for breath and burning up inside.

"Welcome, my man." A junkie leaned across the alleyway, teeth rotted, breath foul. "Welcome to madness, my man."

You could only go so long without sleep, before madness claimed you. Everyone knew that. But everyone knew, deep and low, that along the thread before madness, the toehold before disaster, that was where genius grew

Dax had never been a genius. Had never felt it, within him. Until then.

"Keep going."

Dax was sweating now, bad. You didn't go on the roofs. Bad as it was in the streets, bad as it was in the tunnels, and it was hell bad down there, with the wax always looking for you, the King downbelow claiming his tithe, the sky was worse.

He made it to the top of the ladder, his horn slung across his front to protect it, and swung his good leg cautiously over the edge. His shoe crunched against gravel, the rooftop flat and dry. Dax put more weight down, pretty maybe sure now he wouldn't slip-side right off the rooftop, at least. He looked around, quick-like: a square of gravel glimmering faint and gray, and a figure waiting at the far end, the presence making Dax want to back down the stairs twice as fast as he'd come up, except the golem was climbing behind him, so that wasn't no real option. He turned, looked the other way at the backdrop a thousand more rooftops, some flat, some peaked, some covered in shadows, while others shimmered with lights that made Dax queasy to look at.

So he looked up, instead.

Downbelow, it was all smooth and grey. Streetside, it was all electric lights that didn't show worth a damn, and shadows that did far worse.

Dax had a vague memory of stars, a moon cool white bright, but it didn't particularly surprise him no cool white bright hung over Mad Town. Thick and grey above as it was below, the fairylights on other roofs making it worse instead of better.

The golem hauled itself over the ladder-top, its skin worse for the climb. A long, bloodless tear crossed its square face, and another scored its bare arm. It showed no sign of noticing, as it turned to face Dax again.

"You're stalling."

A muscle in Dax's cheek jumped, and the fingers of his left hand twitched, but the golem was right.

They walked across the rooftop, toward the waiting figure. Dax waited for something to flicker in the corner of his eye, some swooping nightmare or pack of paperboys running the night news. But this corner of Mad City stayed cool and quiet.

Quiet, when it should be chaos? Rooftop didn't even pretend to lawfulness. Things that were out of tune were things to be wary of.

The figure was seated—slumped—in a throne-like chair, darkly-glinting metal in turns and spokes shoved into a shape you could almost sit comfortable in. But the figure in the chair was not comfortable. He shifted, and Dax took a step back, seeing what the shadows had obscured:

The figure was impaled in the chair, spokes through both thighs, and another in his chest.

"I don't know you," Dax said.

The major Nightmares came clear pretty soon after you landed, the ones with real power, the ones who could make hell seem like a better option. You learned and you walked low, and you doffed your cap and kept your tongue still when one of them was around. Lesser nightmares, the paperboys and the waxing-boys, and the pinheads and such, you walked careful 'round but you didn't afear them quite the same.

"Don't you?" Its voice was rough, first guess male but then maybe not, sliding like tuning flute up and down the scale.

Dax put his hands on his horn, and looked this stranger up and down. "No."

It grinned, teeth white as bone shining in the gloaming. "No. No, you don't. You walk right by and you don't see, you glide on by and think you're free. But you're mine. You're mine mine mine."

The voice slid up and down, and despite the disturbing claims—he wasn't nobody's but his own—Dax's fingers itched, the urge to mimic that scale, to improvise on the theme, dig out its joys and fears and turn them into sounds.... Such pain in that voice, and loss, and love and hot-cold orgasmic rhythm.

Wasted, in that withered, crucified frame.

Unable to help himself, Dax touched his horn, fingers curving around the cool metal, bringing it forward and up. Mouth went from dry to soft just thinking about it, and he paused, mouthpiece an inch from his lips. Waiting. Feeling the tension in his bones, the exhaustion of his thoughts, all gather like a cat about to leap.

Here, now. His eyes were too gritty, his mouth too loose. His elbows twinged and his knees shook, his cock standing to attention the first time since he didn't remember when.

"Talk to me," he said. That voice, that voice was the key. "Why am I here?"

Behind them, the golem shifted, stilled.

"Where else would you be? Where else could you be? Alone, only yourself to challenge you to duel, no-one to push your shove."

The voice taunted him, enticed him. Desolation and hope, the push come to shove, the worst anything could be when the only thing that holds you back is nothing at all, the siren song of the unstoppable ego, the thing that got you up on the stage, and Dax, never a fool, no not him, put the horn to his lips and let the voice sink into him, and come back out again.

High notes, shivering down to low, dadadaaaaa… dayum. Dadadaaaaaa… dayum. His body swung, his fingers flew. All the sleepless nights, chasing after that moment, that note, and it had been waiting above him, on the rooftops where nobody went, under a moonless sky…

He no longer played; the horn played him, fingers working the keys, elbows and shoulders moving, his thoughts frozen in the note. The figure leaned forward, the spokes shifting, the entire chair moving as though it were a single entity, and the bone-white teeth flashed again as the fingers settled in Dax's arms, and drew him forward.

Jazz lived in Mad City, in the restless energy, the constant change, the way the Awake flowed through the locals, the nightmares flowed through the Awake, the entire thing sliding around the struts and braces of the Slumbering, improvising its notes out of what it could take from them.

Jazz lived in Mad City, the sleepless vigor, the tight-wound wire, and it rose from the streets and gathered under the clouds and simmered and danced like fairy-lights, waiting. Waiting for a player, a puppet, a bell through which to sound.

LAURA ANNE Gilman is the author of ten *Cosa Nostradamus* novels, including the forthcoming *Dragon Justice,* the Nebula award-nominated *Vineart War* trilogy, and the story collection *Dragon Virus.* A former book editor, her "Practical Meerkat's 52 Bits of Useful Info for Young (and Old) Writers," was published by BookView Press in 2012.

A member of the on-line writers' consortium BookVew Café, Laura Anne now runs an editorial services company, d.y.m.k. productions. Learn more at *lauraannegilman.net* or follow her on Twitter: *@LAGilman*

DON'T LOSE YOUR SON

BY RYAN MACKLIN

I'M NOT A BAD MOTHER. I go to school and work night shift to make a better future for us both. We moved in with Aunt Nancy. I do what I can while for him, but between the night shift at the café and school, I barely see him. And I'm thankful to Aunt Nancy for taking us in. It's hard on him, on us both, but I'm trying to make a better future. A terrible mother would just sit there and let life beat her down.

And a terrible mother wouldn't have rushed into this hellscape to rescue her son. She wouldn't be running from those twisted clown-shaped...things in this place, her son's soul in her bag.

I won't be a terrible mom.

James—the kind, old mechanic that found me when I first came into this place—and I sprinted from the carnival where we'd just taken Timmy's soul. It was a cloudy orange orb. I could feel its warmth radiating from my shoulder bag. It contrasted with the chill of the night air, wet with a drizzle.

Timmy's former captors roared. They weren't far behind.

Behind us, several dozen little clowns gave chase, all angry, hungry, and savage. Each was painted in various bright colors, some with glitter, some in poufy outfits and others in garish jumpsuits. Bozo wigs, moppet hair, clown shoes, all the sorts of things you think of when you think about clowns.

You never think about clowns having sharpened teeth. You never think about them having empty, white eyes.

In front was their leader, Mr. Tickles. It reminded me of those guys from muscle magazine covers. That is, if you just shrunk the body & head, leaving those arms & legs looking even more grotesque and unnatural than they do on a human being. Its fingers ended in bony claws.

Our eyes locked. Orange dripping from the corners of his ghost-white lips. Saliva the same color as Timmy's soul-orb.

Had he already taken a bite...dear god, did he eat...

"This way, Erin!" James pointed left, toward an upcoming street. For an old guy, he made me look slow. I was athletic, and his withered face and thin frame looked more at home in an easy chair than running a marathon.

The street wasn't crowded—people got out of the way as we ran up the street. No, not "people." Men made of shadow and eyes. Boys with knives for fingers. A tall, gaunt woman with hungry eyes and a toothy grin that stretched too wide. Faces familiar from childhood nightmares.

My nightmares took one look at us, and at the oncoming clowns, and fled.

We rounded the corner on to an abandoned side street. It reminded me of San Francisco, a residential block between two major city arteries.

We ran up the block. Mr. Tickles and his clown brood were a couple blocks, maybe three, behind us.

In the back of my mind, I heard a familiar calm, bored voice—me when I was seven—confirm. *Two blocks.*

I took a moment to peek in the bag. The glowing sphere was intact. (I am a good mother and I would figure out how to put my son's soul back.) I don't know much about putting a soul back into a person—hell, I hadn't believed in souls until tonight—but I'd cross that once we were safe.

James lunged at me, trying to pull me or push me or something just as my left foot came down on something other than cobblestone. Cold metal thrust into my flesh.

My foot screamed in pain, and my voice sang its melody.

The old man caught me before I fell into a mouth of shiny, barbed nails. They pulsed and twitched on the surface of the street.

James yanked me back. The street-tooth tore my foot open. He slung my left arm around his shoulder and we hobbled toward a fire escape.

More street-teeth sprang up around us. We hurried as best we could.

Behind us, the clown horde laughed. Mr. Tickles said, his voice like razor wire on a chalkboard, "Give us back our playmate, and you can live." With each word, fingernails scraped the inside of my skull.

Mr. Tickles grinned. The street-teeth stopped coming for us, as he waited for our answer.

James looked around. "Shit," he said under his breath.

Seven-year-old me spoke again inside my head. *Let me play.*

I shut my eyes. Terrible mothers fail their children. Not me. "Okay," I said, concentrating on memories from childhood, from when I was seven, playing with my dolls and their dollhouses. The world started to shift around me.

James shouted, "Erin, don't!"

Everything turned plastic and froze. In that moment, all the pain vanished.

I—not me, but seven year old me, Little-me—looked down at dollhouses and dolls of the buildings along the side street, James & I, the clowns, everything down to lampposts and even the street-teeth.

Little-me frowned at the clowns. She (I? Maybe we?) scooped them up and threw them into the trash can at her feet. She put James and I on a roof, and gathered all the toothy cobblestones into the trash before putting us back down.

I could see more around her and the dollhouses on top of the dresser. We were in my bedroom from years and years ago. So many toys. One for every secret Dad wanted me to keep.

Little-me reached inside the sock drawer and dug around, until her hand touched cool metal. Dad's old Zippo. I used to steal it from him all the time.

She lit everything in the trash can on fire.

Such horrible, high-pitched screams and wails. Pleas of mercy form tinny voice boxes made of now-melting plastic ended in gurgles. Burned plastic and ozone filled my nostrils.

Little-me stared down at doll-me. *Let's keep playing,* she whispered and she eyed the buildings, the lighter still lit.

"No."

Her eyes narrowed at me.

"Not now, okay?" I reasoned.

The lighter clicked close, and I opened my eyes. Everyone but James was gone. We were in the middle of the street, now bare, with the rain starting to...

Everything went white as I screamed, the pain rushing back in like a river breaking a levy. I fell to the ground, scraping my palms. I got lucky; I didn't land on the bag with my son's orb.

James rushed over and helped me sit. "Erin," he said quietly, "are you okay?"

I couldn't answer. Somewhere in the back of my mind, I registered the sensation of heavier rain. I focused on that as best I could.

James fished inside the bag and got the orb out. "Damn it, Erin." He turned it around in his hands, and held it in front of my face.

Oh dear God, there was a crack in it.

Words fought to come out of my mouth, and they all failed to do anything but sputter in panic.

He put his other hand gently on my shoulder. "We can't go around using our powers around souls. They're delicate and what we do isn't."

My head cleared as he talked. The pain moved from dominating to being a background roar.

James looked me up and down. "We can't get anywhere with your foot like that."

I didn't want to look at how bad it was, so I looked up at the sky. Faint light reflected off the off of the clouds in the starless void this world called a sky.

He stood up and peered north, toward the giant clock tower in the center of the city. "An hour till the door back to your place closes. Won't be closed long, but I doubt you'll survive the hunt to see it open again."

From a bit off in the distance, a tinny clown-voice shouted. "Timmy! We want to keep playing!"

My eyes widened. I grabbed James' shirt. Pain for a moment, replaced by the sweet kiss of panic's adrenaline. "I thought…"

He cut me off as he helped me stand. "Mr. Tickles can't be stopped that easy, kiddo." He helped me hobble to a manhole. "Can't make it on the surface. But he won't follow us underground."

"Isn't that worse? I've heard stories."

"They're true. But we're not going to make it like this." He grabbed and lifted the manhole cover with one hand, like it was the lid to a jar.

A smell wafted up from below—slightly sweet, fresh, like daisies and cotton candy.

"We're just going to walk a few blocks," said James. "I know a safe place."

He gestured at the ladder, and I swung down, my good foot finding purchase. My left foot hung in space as I climbed down, even with no pressure on it just as excruciating as stepping on something. It throbbed and pulsed, my personal beacon of torment. But I fought through it. I couldn't fail Timmy.

I'm not a terrible mom.

The round sewer corridor was empty, save for us. Large candles hung down from the ceiling every few feet, casting dim light down both directions. Instead of water, melted wax flowed down. Different colored orbs drifted inside the wax river—souls and memories of innocent people. While James climbed down behind me, all I could do was stare at them.

That's where the scent came from.

We continued down the sewer walkway in silence. My eyes drifted to the orbs, each one looked so much like Timmy's.

They all need a good mom to save them.

I didn't respond to Little-me. But she knew that I wanted to do something, even if I wasn't exactly sure what that something was. That didn't matter; Timmy was more important than these souls.

We can come back tomorrow night.

I didn't respond, but I didn't dismiss the thought, either.

James and I were crossing a little arched bridge at a river intersection, when he stopped short .

The hairs on the back of my neck stood up.

"What?" I whispered.

He looked back the way we came. "They know we're here." He walked backward a few feet, and my good foot followed.

"They?"

At that moment, I heard the clomping sound of heavy steps and two wax-covered horsemen walked into view from around a corner.

No, not horsemen. Each had the head of a horse, but the body of a man. Like living chess pieces. Each wore armor like in the movies, huge suits of metal and helmets that covered most of their faces. In each eye was a candle flame. Their swords were made of wax, but still promised danger.

"Halt, Shaper James." The horseman's voice echoed harsh and commanding in the tunnel.

"We mean you no harm or ill, Knights of Wax." James gave a shallow bow.

They bowed in return. "As the friend of the King, you have passage in His domain, Shaper. Your companion, however, does not. She must pay a toll, and His Majesty tasked us to collect."

I felt the stare of their candle-eyes on my bag.

My fists balled up, ready for a fight. *Let's play again*, she sang in my mind. I shoved her away for now—Timmy might not survive another crack.

I was not going to let them take Timmy away from me without what little fight I could give.

James squeezed my shoulder gently. "My good knights, this is Lady Erin, newly Awake."

They paused, hands on the hilts of their wax-swords, but not tightly. Like a cop putting his hand on his gun to tell you who's in control. I remembered my ex pulling that. "We had heard of a new arrival to the City. You know that The Wax King requires a meeting with all Awake traveling in His domain. Come, we will escort you."

"She's in no condition to travel."

"That does not concern us. You will meet with Him." Their grips tightened and their swords tasted the air in front of us.

Wax dripped off of the blades. I heard a sizzle from the ground.

James said something. I don't know what he said. My vision blurred. My good leg fell out from under me. I heard murmuring, I think, I don't know. Huh, is my cheek on the sewer floor? I thought it would be colder to the touch.

I was jerked up. A slap to the face.

"Erin!" Someone shouted.

Another slap to the face. My eyes opened.

"Thank god!"

The light was dim. The sweet smell from before told me that we were in the sewer. Or maybe Heaven.

My eyes focused. It was James. He was covered in cuts and wax. Once he saw my eyes focus on him, he helped me to my feet.

"Surface. Now."

I thought "Okay," but the word never escaped my lips. He had me wrap my arms around his neck while he climbed up the ladder. I looked down below—not by choice, but my head flopped to the side, having no spare energy to hold it up. Floating in the wax were pieces of horse-knight.

Little-me looked down at this and furrowed her brow. She wanted to play with them, and now they were gone. I suppose that was James' handiwork, but I wasn't really sure what he exactly did. He never told me what black gift the nightmares gave him.

Wait.

Timmy.

I didn't go wide-eyed or panic; there was no energy left in me to do so. I whispered a prayer, asking God to please let Timmy be okay, to not have another crack in his orb from whatever it was that James did. Please, dear God, please.

He lifted the manhole cover and pushed it over, climbing out with me on him. We came into an alley, warehouses on either side. James carried me on his back and kicked one of the doors open.

Stench hit us in the face like a fist. It stuck in my nose, like lard and dog vomit mixed together, that'd been left in the sun, and smeared in my nostrils. It covered the inside of my throat like an unwelcome blanket in summer, sticky and hot. I could feel it on my tongue.

I threw up on James' neck.

We kept moving, up some stairs and through a door. The smell dramatically eased as we moved through the building. After a couple more heavy doors, I couldn't smell it anymore. Then pain went back to the forefront.

He laid me down on a desk, then took my bag. "I'll be right back, Erin. Shit. Don't lose any more blood."

The room spun. I shut my eyes to keep the dizzy feeling at bay. On the bright side, I didn't feel much pain anymore. I barely registered, a thought, that that probably wasn't a good thing.

An eternity later, he came back.

"Ja—"

"Hang on, kiddo." He grabbed my bad foot and raised it up ripping the cloth around my calf. It was swollen and purple. Half of my foot was gone, rotted off, and the other half was black and withered. Pus oozed from the end of my foot.

Panic set in. My foot's missing. I shouted random syllables, in a birdshot approach to forming words.

James seemed to get my attempt at a message. "Erin, calm down. This'll be over in a moment."

I thrashed with what little energy I could muster, but it wasn't enough.

James grabbed my leg hard and I screamed. Only for a moment, then my throat was hoarse. I could feel myself screaming, but sound didn't come out. He sunk his hands into my calf, his fingers two knuckles deep into my flesh. Those hands raked up my leg to my battered foot, scraping across bone and pushing bits of me around. It was like shards of glass were ripping into bit of my calf and feet as his hands slowly moved to my foot, the fingers twitching around inside my leg, dancing and darting around.

Hot tears welled in my eyes. All I could think was how much of a release death would bring.

Then, nothing. The pain faded, all of it. My head started to clear, and energy returned. James offered a hand and a smile. It took me a moment to decide if I could trust him, but I grabbed and he helped me up.

"How do you feel?"

I looked down at my foot. My new, intact foot. Shiny skin, like you see in commercials when someone uses some youth-restoring cream, but this was the real deal. My shoe was torn to hell, but I wiggled my toes and everything felt normal. I just nodded at him.

As I kicked off my torn shoe and then the whole one, I saw that James didn't have the bag on him. It wasn't in the room anywhere. "Where is he?" I spat.

"Couldn't do what I just did around the orb. You know."

I hopped to my feet and walked beside him. "What about in the sewer?"

His eyes met mine for just a moment, and darted away. He said nothing. I said nothing. Every mother has seen time and time again the way shame changes how someone stands—how your shoulders sink down, your eyes staring vacantly at the ground, the shallow neck swallows, all of those little things.

I exhaled. "Is he okay?"

"I didn't look. I found a hiding place , where Mr. Tickles couldn't smell it out. Then came back here."

I nodded.

"But I..." James stopped after I put my hand up.

"Show me where."

We left the room. The stench started to come back, but faint. He moved through some halls, and I followed. This place was like the inside corridors of a mall: gray, grimy, cold, and wide enough for a cart to drive through.

James took me to a small door labeled "Aging," in letters that were made by someone cutting steel with a hot blade. He hesitated before opening the door.

My eyes shut. The putrid stench hit again, like a fire hose to my face. James ran in. I gave it a moment before I did the same, looking inside where I was about to enter.

Before me was a large, double-story space, big enough to hold a couple planes I guess. There were meat hooks in the ceiling. Each held a ghostly image of a man, woman, girl or boy, the hook piercing their necks, a glowing ichor dripping from them into buckets placed underneath. They twitched and looked like they were screaming or moaning, yet they were silent.

Bile filled my mouth. It was the first time I even had bile taste far better than what triggered it.

James was on the floor, waving me down. I ran in, down the battered wooden stairs and across to where he was, next to a pile of those ghostly bodies. He pushed the top of the pile around. They shrieked with each touch.

I just stared at the pile. At the children.

The Little-me knew what I was thinking. *Let's take them all home.*

"Not now," I whispered. James' arm emerged from the pile with the bag, dripping with glowing ichor. I snatched it from his hands and opened it.

Timmy was flickering, fading.

With the bag in hand, I ran toward the normal door next to the giant rolling one. As I opened it my bare feet touched the rough, unkind surface of an alley. The manhole nearby still had its cover off. This was where we came in from.

I heard that high-pitched shout from not too far away. Maybe a couple blocks. Mr. Tickles.

"I smell him, boys! This way!"

James ran up next to me. "Which way?" I screamed more than asked.

He pointed down one end of the alley. "Turn left. Run a few blocks. You'll recognize the building." I started to take off, but he wasn't by my side. I looked back, and he ran the other direction, toward the horde.

"What the hell?"

"I'm gonna buy you some time, kiddo." He disappeared around the corner. I kept on.

"James, don't be a fool!" I grabbed his arm. He was about to throw himself to the wolves.

Worse, I was about to face what else this city had in story for me alone.

He yanked back. "Run, Erin!"

My body tensed up, half of me ready to sprint, half of me too scared. I wouldn't have gotten this far without him.

"Come on, James!"

"No!" The horde sounded closer. "You remember those souls in the sewer? People stolen from the real world. And those knights? That's what I do. I turn innocent people into monsters."

The tension in my body left, my mind turned to processing…no, wait, no…

"Parents don't come for them, and if I don't do it, someone else will. So I buy my freedom with their souls."

My mouth opened, but I had no words.

"Run, you fucking moron!" The clown horde was at the mouth of the alley. So many, ready to rip us into red mist and flesh confetti.

The last thing I saw before I ran were his eyes. They began to split apart. Mandibles slowly protruded from his mouth, glistening. That was all I needed to see. Whatever he was about to do, Timmy couldn't be around for it.

Shit, neither could I.

I took off, sprinting as fast as I could, dodging the nightmare denizens milling about. More shadow men, hulking brutes made of muscle and malice, toddlers covered in teeth and maws. I flowed around them, dodging and keeping from reach.

They didn't try to grab, but their eyes we all on me. And they smiled, as if to say they were going to enjoy the show.

As I ran, the horde sounded farther away. There was a roar, a lion's roar, giant, large enough to be a house. I took a peek back and saw an orange mane poking out from above the roofs. Clowns were on it, biting and stabbing.

Snapped my head forward, focusing on the road. I turned right after a couple blocks, following along toward the clock tower. The house was nearby.

As I did, I heard a wail. The ground shook. I don't know how I knew, but I felt a pressure form behind me, and I knew James lost.

God damn this fucking place.

I heard that voice again, Mr. Tickles, echo around me. "Get her!" With that, street-teeth came up just before my next step.

There was a parked car nearby—something you'd see in a movie set in the 20s. I jumped onto it, and my feet felt leather, not steel. I jumped from car to car, avoiding the stretch of teeth. My foot landed on the truck of the third car, onto a bump.

Out of reflex, I looked down. A nose. A face. I stepped on a face.

Was everything here made out of good, lost people?

I ran out of cars to climb on, but the sidewalk was clear. I didn't trust that, but I didn't have a choice. After another half-block up, I turned a corner, my aching legs pumping, feet stinging from the rocks and glass, but I didn't slow. My old building was ahead, just a couple more minutes and I'd be home.

The building looked like my crappy, drafty four-story Victorian, but where the paint flaked and peeled, it showed bone underneath rather than wood. The building swayed in the wind and grunted with each movement.

The street was empty. Just me, Timmy, and my goal.

The roar of the clown horde came from the intersection ahead. They swarmed on to the street.

I scanned for some way to get over them, a fire escape ladder or windows to climb, anything. But the clowns were everywhere. No way past.

Mr. Tickles walked slowly toward me. I stopped running, not sure where to go. All momentum and adrenaline fled my body as I stopped moving.

"You can't have him!" My voice betrayed my exhaustion.

Mr. Tickles giggled as it kept slowly walking forward, orange drool dripping from its mouth. The street around me bubbled and became soft. My feet sank into quicksand.

"Silly girl," it squeaked, "playtime is over." That grin. Those teeth. All of the clowns surrounding me, eager to pounce.

Playtime isn't over yet. Little-me was a vicious brat.

I looked down into the bag. Spider web cracks covered its flickering surface, but there was still light in it.

I nodded, and the world froze again into Little-me's dollhouse view. She picked me up, opened the roof of the horror-mirror

Victorian, and put me inside Timmy's room, next to the doorway back to the real world.

But she wasn't done.

"No!" I mind-screamed my legs frozen to doll-plastic. But Little-me shook her head.

Bad men need to go away.

She dumped rubbing alcohol all over the clowns and lit them on fire. And she stood there, watching the plastic figures on her dresser burn and melt, all while I was frozen, a doll in her world.

"Let me go, Erin. I need to get Timmy home." I would have cried if I was flesh right then.

She looked at me, looked back at the burning pile of clowns, and then picked up the still-aflame Mr. Tickles.

Little-me's eyes glowed red, her face angry and bitter. She grabbed a hammer and, while it was burning her hand, she held it in place and beat it to pieces. Then she turned back to me, and her eyes cooled.

I was in control, and looking out again through my own eyes. The shrieks of hundreds of burning clown-things filled the sky.

In front of me was Timmy's closet, the doorway where Mr. Tickles had come through to steal Timmy's soul, and where I ran to give chase. The clock tower was chiming and the door was closing.

I dove through the closet. Everything behind me went silent. It was dark on the other side. I could feel carpet on my palms.

A car alarm went off in the distance. A normal, everyday car alarm. I exhaled, suddenly feeling the weight of exhaustion on me.

It was a trial to stand up. I wanted to just collapse on the floor. The idea of carpet was the most comfortable, divine thing I'd encountered in the last few days. "A few more minutes, then you can," I told myself.

Timmy, lay in his bed, where he was when I left. He still held onto his bunny rabbit doll. His breathing was shallow. I sat in the chair next to his bed, just like I did night after night reading stories to him.

The streetlight shone on his sweet little face.

I opened up the bag and took out the orb. There was barely any light coming out of it, and it felt like lukewarm water. Orange goo dribbled from one of the cracks, and I rotated it to try to keep what was left inside.

"Please," I prayed as I gently took the stuffed animal from his arms. When I put the orb in its place, it dissolved and drifted inside of him. He didn't stir. He still breathed, his chest going up and down, but it didn't stir. I thought about waking him up, but I...no, maybe it just takes time to heal. I let him stay asleep.

I put the bunny back in his arms and tucked the blanket over him. Then I sat back and let my eyes close.

But sleep didn't come. Only tears.

When **RYAN MACKLIN** isn't pondering ways to torture protagonists, he spends his days as a freelance writer and editor, and his nights as a geek deconstructing novels & movies. He's written & edited a few award-winning games, including the ***Dresden Files Roleplaying Game***. And when Ryan's taking a breather, he's probably playing some console RPG or weird indie game.

His blog and links to other projects can be found at: *RyanMacklin.com.* Follow him on Twitter: *@RyanMacklin.*

DON'T IGNORE YOUR DEAD

BY MONICA VALENTINELLI

I'M AT A DINER HOVERING OVER ANOTHER CUP of burnt coffee and a pile of slimy pancakes covered in syrup. Yesterday, my landlord kicked me out of my apartment. I can't say I blame the old lady. She needs the rent and I want the power to bring back the dead. Money's tight because the insurance company is *still* investigating the accident. If I'm guilty, I'll wind up in jail.

Even though the cops say they're done questioning me, it's been hard to focus. Every time I close my eyes, I see a bloody hand. It's not mine, but most days I wish it was.

I dump another sugar packet into my coffee and hope the caffeine will help me wake up. So far, it's not helping.

What if her death *was* my fault? What if the reason my baby sister was killed, was because I swerved left instead of right?

I don't remember much since her funeral, but what I can picture clearly is our last morning together—right up to the part where the airbags exploded.

The accident happened over Christmas break. I had just gotten my license back after one too many speeding tickets and wanted to take my dad's car out for a spin. It was supposed to be a quick errand.

In and out. Grab a gallon of milk, a box of cookies, and some diapers. That's it.

Only, Dad wouldn't let me drive alone.

"*Raven, you're not going to be home very long,*" Dad reminded me using his stern oh-so-serious voice. "*Just spend some time with her before you head back to school. Okay?*"

"*Fine, then I'm taking the SUV.*" I remember rolling my eyes at him. I don't know why I was annoyed, I just was. Dad knew it, too.

"*Do you want to drive or not?*"

"*Going!*"

I must have been in a girly mood because I dressed my sister like a doll. Her outfit was a pink monstrosity with a matching headband and frilly socks. She was in a good mood that morning and didn't fuss or squirm—not even when I buckled her into the car seat.

After five minutes on the road, she was out cold and started to snore. Ten minutes later and …

My sister was killed a few stoplights away from the grocery store. I remember getting into the left hand lane, putting my signal on, and stepping on the gas when I saw the green light. I couldn't tell the police what I was wearing that day or if it was raining. I just remember turning left.

Then? I saw the truck.

I must have done something to avoid the crash because the next thing I knew the SUV rolled, the airbags deployed, and I hit my head. If I had met that semi head on, I'd be dead, too.

When I regained consciousness, I found myself lying in a hospital bed. The first question I asked was about my baby sister. "Is she all right?"

The nurse patted my hand, filled me back up with pain meds, and told me everything was going to be okay. "Just rest now, Raven. Your sister's in good hands."

She lied.

An hour later, the cops arrived. Their first inquiry was: *Would I identify the body?*

I nodded without saying a word.

The nurse helped me out of bed and escorted me to the morgue. I charged through the swinging doors and flew to my sister's side. When I saw her tiny frame I knelt down, wrapped her bloody fingers around my thumb, and cried until I had nothing left. I barely even registered there were other people in the room. All I wanted was my sister. Alive.

Second question: *Did I steal the car?*

I laughed at their stupid accusation. My dad and I didn't share the same last name. Divorced, remarried, and divorced again—but he was still my dad.

Did I have permission to drive?

I confessed I did. Then, the cops shook their heads and told me there'd be a major investigation. There was a good possibility I'd be charged with vehicular manslaughter.

At first, I didn't understand what they were saying.

"Wait!" When I realized what they were accusing me of, I puked all over the shiny floor. "You *can't* ... I didn't kill... I *love*—"

Make sure you get a good lawyer.

My dad was waiting in the hallway outside. He wouldn't— *couldn't*—look me in the eye.

"I'm sorry, Dad. It was an accident!"

The words *"I'm sorry!"* fell from my lips a thousand times but he wasn't listening. My baby sister (and his new daughter) was gone. Never mind the damage to the car. Machines can be broken, fixed, and replaced. People? Families? No band aid or anti-depressant can heal the pain caused by the death of someone you love.

I found that out the hard way.

"Something wrong with your cakes, honey?" I don't mean to, but I make a face when my waitress hovers over me. Her presence reminds me I have no place else to go. She reeks of cigarette smoke and kitchen grease. "You want me to send them back?"

"No, no..." I dump a forkful of mush into my mouth and give her the thumbs up. She could have booted me out of the restaurant hours ago, but she didn't. "They're grwaflt!"

The waitress smiles and pats me on the head. "I remember what it's like to be young. Stay off the drugs and you'll be all right."

"Sure."

"Though, you might want to think twice about getting any more tattoos ..."

She claims they're tattoos. I call them "battle scars."

I force the lump of wet dough down my throat and concentrate on my plate, hoping she'll annoy somebody else. "They're good."

"Glad to hear it!" Before she wanders off, she says: "Hey, you work for that insurance company up the road?"

My whole body stiffens and my fork slips right out of my hand. "No, I don't have a job right now. Why do you want to know?"

"I hear they're hiring." Part of me wants the waitress to shut the hell up; the other part wonders why she's so nice to me. Doesn't she know I'm a killer?

"Yeah? What could I do for a company like that?"

Then, the waitress winks at me and says something strange. "Breakfast is on me, kiddo."

"Thanks." As soon as she turns around, I slump down in my chair, and cover my face. Questions worm their way into the back of my skull. *Did anybody recognize me? How badly do I want that file? Will I get caught stealing it?*

What else do I have left to lose?

While the cops were anxious to close the case, they obligated to do their due diligence since I was a minor. The investigation after the accident proceeded in the most bureaucratic way possible—slow, and at the mercy of everyone else's schedule. There were too many questions and not enough witnesses.

At the time, my dad said I could stay with him for a while. He forced me to deal with the logistics of all the funeral arrangements and the insurance claim prep.

I thought I was doing all right until I started dealing with Brubaker Life and Accidental Insurance. In addition to several interviews and pictures of the car, they requested a death certificate. Then? An autopsy and a certified death certificate. After that, they asked for another copy to send to their home office. Did my sister have any pre-existing medical conditions? Did her mother pass down any genetic defects? Was she small for her age? Did the family have a history of mental illness? Was I suffering from insomnia?

I snort, gulp my now-tolerable (but cold) coffee, and inhale a couple of sugar packets. I did not have insomnia then, but I certainly do now. I stopped sleeping right after I told my Dad I might be a murderer.

"*Dad?*"

He'd been drinking. Again. "*Get out.*"

"*Daddy?*" Drunk or sober, I needed him. I couldn't go back to school until the cops cleared my name and I didn't have much money left, either. "*What's going on?*"

"*I told them you didn't have permission.*"

At first, I thought he had been replaced by an alien. After my sister died, my father changed into someone mean, sad, and distant. I barely recognized him. "*Why... Why would you say that? That wasn't true!*"

"*For the insurance. The neighbors said I'd have a better chance of getting the claim paid if you took the car on your own.*"

"*I don't care about the money. I could wind up in jail because of you!*" I stepped right in front of my father and he turned his back to me. "*Please, help me.*"

His words were flat, foreign. "*Like you helped your sister?*"

I recognized my father's grief had affected his judgment, but that just made me feel worse. Since I couldn't argue with him, my survival instincts took over. "*I could use some rent money. I have some savings, but I need enough for a deposit.*"

"*On the table.*" Dad pointed to an overstuffed piggy bank. "*Your sister's college fund.*"

"*Ouch.*"

Ignoring me, my father grabbed his keys and headed for the door. "*I don't want you to be here when I get back.*"

I slam my fist down on the restaurant table. The memory of the pain plastered all over my dad's face makes me angry. If it wasn't for that damn insurance company, I'd still have a father. I'd still have a home.

I grab a couple of bucks out of my pocket and toss them on a clean spot. The insurance company isn't that far away. I'm so pissed off I march to the gas station, stuff my pockets full of junk food, and march right to their front door.

The company's headquarters don't impress me. One of the front windows is cracked and the red paint on their sign is peeling. Once I'm inside, I notice the reception area is even worse. The carpeting reeks of mold and rotten roses.

"Back again?" The woman sitting at the circular front desk doesn't look familiar. "It's like I told you before Miss Bird. The adjusters are working on your claim—"

"I've never met you before." I shake my head, frustrated that I've been mistaken for someone else.

"Well, Miss Bird—"

"—Raven. Ray like the singer. Venn like the diagram."

"Whatever," the woman rolls her eyes and adjusts her thick glasses. She reminds me of a faded picture I once saw of my mother. I never met her, but I hate her, too. Dear old mom didn't bother showing up to my sister's funeral. "Why don't you leave your name and number in the guest book and someone will call you back. Remember what I told you last week? We have procedures to follow."

I fold my arms across my chest. I am not buying any of this woman's bullshit. Not today. "Angry secretary is it?"

"My *name* is Catherine, but you may call me *Miss* Parker."

"Fine, Miss Parker. Why don't you get a rep up here? I promised the police I'd get them something today."

That's only half-true. Cops said they had what they needed, but for me? The law's not enough. I want my father back.

"Now just see here Miss Bird—"

"Raven."

"Miss Raven. We've been cooperating with the police. I know how hard this must be for you, but until our adjusters finish their investigation, I can't let you talk to them. Though, I have to wonder why you're here …"

That gets my attention. "What do you mean? Are they still going to arrest me? It's been over two months!"

"I don't know if I'm the right person to tell you what happened. I suggest you call the police." Catherine shoots me a quizzical look, presses a button, and types something into the computer. "Now I must ask you to leave before I call Security."

"Security?" All I want is the truth but that, like so many other details, was cloudy. I don't remember talking to this woman before. Was she lying to me? "Catherine, you're full of surprises."

"Get some sleep, Raven." Disappointment splatters across her broad face. Both of her chins wag. "You look like hell."

"Bathroom?"

Kate points, then turns back to her monitor. "Down the hall, just like last time."

I salute Catherine Parker, receptionist extraordinaire, and take my leave. I avoid the restroom. Instead, I sneak around the corner and shut myself into a nearby janitor's closet. I would wait all day if I had to.

One way or another I was going to get that damn file.

The dark safety of the janitor's closet allows me to close my eyes and rest. My dreams are plagued with nightmares of flying pigs and giant trucks.

When I wake up, I notice is that my body doesn't hurt as bad as it normally does. Weird. I stretch, then scarf down a protein bar and pull out my phone. *Two-thirty a.m.* Later than I thought.

After two energy shots and a bag of candy, I tiptoe past the front desk and wind through a maze of brown cubicles. My destination? A wall of filing cabinets.

The place is empty. I thought there'd be someone else around, like a cleaning lady, but I guess I'm a little paranoid. Still, something's not right. Either I'm really tired or my eyesight is starting to go. My vision is blurry, like someone took an eraser to the edges.

"You're acting like a moron, Raven."

After I convince myself I have nothing to be afraid of, I run straight up to a drawer marked "Yoast to Yurick" and flip through its contents. The file for claimant Edward C. Young is pretty thick. My hands tremble as I pull it out. *This is it.* Whatever's in this file will bring my father back. He can't ignore me now.

Now all I need is proof.

I wander over to a large copier and press a button. It hums to life. The file has a ton of papers in it; I wish I could speed up the process.

Grrrrrrrrrrrr ...

Wait. Was that a growl? Am I *still* dreaming? I pinch myself and it hurts. Guess not. Maybe I need glasses or a hearing aid. More sleep couldn't hurt, either.

Tssssssssshhhhhhk.

I recognize that sound. It's coming from *inside* the copy machine. I pop the lid and peer into the glass. Time slows. I can count the seconds, but I can't see why the copier's acting up. I slide behind it and reach for the plug when—

Oh, shit. "Is someone there?"

Tsshhhhhk. Ssshhhhhk.

I don't remember pressing any buttons.

"Come on, now. Is this a joke?" I whirl around and face myself. I'm not sure *how* it happened, but somehow the machine figured out a way to create a life-size facsimile of … *me*.

Instead of combat boots, Raven Number Two is wearing Mary Janes.

Her hair is dull brown, not pink.

She's wearing a summery dress. It's strapless and it has tiny blue flowers on it.

Her skin is golden, like she just stepped out of the sun, but that's not the freakiest part. It's her arms. They're bare.

No tattoos.

"No battle scars!" I cry. "You're not real. What are you?"

Tsshhhhhk. Ssshhhhhk.

Thick, gray smoke pours out of the copier, filling the air. Raven Number Two turns sideways, folds herself in half, and slides back into the tray. The lid shuts and a new image is copied over the old one. It's another picture of me. Only this time she's …

That can't be right. Raven Number Three has my trench coat on, her pink hair is spiked up, and her nose and eyebrows are pierced.

Tsshhhhhk. Ssshhhhhk.

That sound. That terrible, unforgiving sound! I can't tear my eyes away. I don't dare.

A piece of paper flies out and lands at my feet. An image of my own hand lifts off the page and reaches out for me. I shriek. What do I do? Run? Fight? I just wanted to copy the file, not throw down with *myself*.

The truth is: I'm exhausted. Right here, right now *this* is where I finally get whatever's coming to me for killing my sister. No cops, no grieving father, no awful receptionist.

"What do you want?" I shout at Raven Number Three. "Are you going to kill me? Is that it? Drag me with you? Papercut me to death?"

At first, Raven Number Three doesn't answer me. She leans against the wall staring at me with flat black eyes and a twisted mouth. Then, she raises a finger and points at the copier. It glows bright, bright red and emits a high-pitched whirring sound.

"No more! Do you hear me?"

Raven Number Three blows me a kiss, flips the lid, and slips back inside.

Tssshhhh-shhhhhk.

The question printed on the next sheet is the same one I've been asking myself for weeks.

ARE YOU SURE YOU'RE INNOCENT?

Tssshhhh-shhhhhk.

YOU'RE CARELESS, RAVEN. IT'LL HAPPEN AGAIN.

I know what she's—*I'm*—hinting at. "What? What happens again?"

Tssshhhh-shhhhhk.

My whole body quivers. The copier not only understands what I'm saying—it is communicating with me. I wave the smoke away and inspect the scanner; a pair of red eyes glares back at me. Then, the imprint of a hand presses on the underside of the glass. Not my hand, a baby's hand. It's clean and pink and healthy.

My sister can't still be alive. Can she?

Tssshhhh-shhhhhk.

THIRD MESSAGE: TELL HER THE TRUTH.

"You don't know what you're saying." I spit at the ground. "Who the fuck are you to tell me that? I didn't take your life. You're just an office copier."

Tssshhhh-shhhhhk.

I WAS PROUD TO BE YOUR SISTER.

"Elisabeth? Is that really you?" I fall on my knees and clasp my hands. It *can't* be her. But what if … What if it *is?*

I close my eyes and try to focus. All this time, I've been dealing with everything *but* my sister's death. What's a file or a check compared to her memory? I couldn't even say her name out loud. Elisabeth. "Forgive me, baby girl. Please? Even if the accident wasn't my fault, I'm sorry. I'm so sorry I didn't protect you. I promise I'll get my shit together, okay?"

I hear a series of popping noises, then a loud *poof.*

"I love you, Elisabeth."

When I open my eyes, everything jumps back into focus and there's no trace of Raven Number Two, Three or Elisabeth. The only evidence I have that I'm not completely insane is the smell of burnt rubber, the toner now covering my hands and legs, and several pieces of paper lying all around me.

I force myself to pick one of them up. The sheets are not blank and the messages are still intact. That's when I know: I have to read the file. Clean myself up? Fix things with my dad? Not possible. Not completely. Even if I'm found innocent, all of my imperfections—like my insomnia—are part of who I am. I can move forward, but I will never, ever change what happened.

"This is the police. Turn around. Slowly."

"The police? When did you get here?" My thoughts race as I try to buy more time. Why didn't I just read the damn file and leave? I pretend nothing's wrong. "Is there a problem?"

For a few seconds, no one says a word. Then, a familiar face pops into view: "Raven? I want you to cooperate with the police, okay? We'll figure this out."

"Daddy?" I want to run into his arms and ask him to take me home, but I don't. Instead, I say: "I got the file."

"I've been trying to call you all day, but you must have changed your number."

His words bring tears to my eyes. "Yeah, I had to ditch my smart phone. This is pre-paid. Guess I forgot to let you know."

"The other driver was arrested yesterday afternoon."

"Oh, God." I collapse to the floor and wrap my skinny arms around my body. I am innocent. I am not going to prison for killing my sister. I am not a murderer.

"And the claim?"

"Well, that's my fault. I still have to clear things up on my own. I want you to come home, okay?"

"You mean you forgive me?"

Dad reaches for my hand and pulls me off the dusty carpet. "I'm sorry, Raven. I haven't forgotten about you."

I sniffle and hug him fiercely. "How can you, Dad? I'm the only daughter you've got left."

The police loom behind us, waiting to arrest me. I stand up and they start to read me my rights. Not for killing my sister, but for trespassing.

"Wait!" I turn to the copier one, last time. "Just …"

"Take it easy." My dad throws his hands up, trying to protect me from the fidgety cops. "Can't you give me and my daughter a break? She didn't even leave the building."

While my dad is arguing with the police, I bend over the machine, and whisper good-bye. "Rest in peace, Elisabeth."

Tssshhhh-shhhhhk.

Sleep well, Raven.

"I will, sis. I promise."

As we head toward the front door, a comforting thought enters my mind: no matter where I end up, I am finally free.

MONICA VALENTINELLI is an author and game designer who lurks in the dark. Her publications include nonfiction, original and tie-in fiction. Stories range from *Redwing's Gambit,* a novella set in the universe of the *Bulldogs!* RPG, and "Tailfeather" which debuted in *Apexology: Science Fiction and Fantasy.* In addition to her short stories, novellas, articles, and RPG contributions, Monica crafted one of the first enhanced e-books titled *The Queen of Crows.* In her spare time, she dons the role of project manager for horror and dark fantasy webzine, *FlamesRising.com*.

For more about Monica and her work, visit her website at: *www.mlvwrites.com*

DON'T LEAVE YOUR LOVE

BY WILL HINDMARCH

SHE HEARD THE GEARS LOCK INTO PLACE. She heard the tower toll. Once, twice. Her feet hit the pavement on the third and fourth strikes. On the fifth and sixth she stumbled, asphalt worn away to cobbles beneath, exposed bones. On the seventh toll she peered around the street corner toward her target. On the eighth, she peered back over her shoulder.

Nine, ten. Except for newspaper pages drifting, the street was empty. Stark colorless streetlamps lit a wet avenue. Above them, dark shapes of awnings and scaffolds. Above that, the skyline. White squares of light in black buildings against a sky foggy and two-toned as a used blackboard.

At the eleventh toll, she sprinted around the corner. She was already too late. She ran anyway.

At the twelfth, she patted the pockets of her leather coat. Two small packages, still intact.

At the thirteenth toll she saw him move at the rendezvous. His shape reflected in the wet pavement. He turned in her direction, arms at his side, tilted his head.

That final toll echoed back off the city. She imagined herself running through the echo as it passed over her like a sheet of rain. Her footfalls echoed, high black boots on patched potholes.

She heard the echoes. The Nightmares could, too.

He waited at the foot of the building like she'd told him. He looked pale in his sweater and pea coat. His light hair wafted in the pre-rain.

From the outside, it was a ragged monument of a building—once pretty, once rich, now all alone in a row of cob-webbed tenements and vacant office towers. Its fine adornments, its lustrous glass, its plush décor, were left out in the rain and the soot so long that the whole building looked like it had been forgotten in some basement. Gray water stains ran down its white façade like smeared mascara. Curtains rippled out of broken windows like waving ghosts.

The front of the place was anchored by revolving doors, locked and smashed. Broken windowpanes looked like shark's teeth. The ground floor choked on boards and barricades.

She knew how to get inside: the way she'd gotten out. She first entered the city through a door on the top floor—the 12th floor—and she hoped the door was still there. She pried away boards to get out through the corner entrance, at the restaurant, beneath a turret that hung over the sidewalk. That part of the building was granite. It made up the base of the building, above which floor after floor of white stone on gray stone were stacked. All of it topped with a spiny, Gothic crown. Soaring verticality. It drew the eye up.

She grabbed him by the arm, barely slowing as she passed. "Come on," she said.

He followed along, taking her hand. Didn't say anything.

"You got here okay," she asked.

He nodded, looking still in the direction she'd come from as he moved with her. They dashed the length of the building, turned at the corner and climbed the wide stone steps under the heavy turret to the corner door. The turret seemed too heavy to stay aloft forever, its back up against the building like that.

She held a finger up to him, equal parts "wait" and "quiet." She went back to the corner of the door's nouveau archway and peered back the way they'd come.

A black dog stood in the street, right where he'd been waiting for her. Not a Doberman, not a Rottweiler. Three feet tall. All black. Eyes like perfect round reflectors, shining bright, though it wasn't that close to the lamp. It raised its head, sniffed the air.

She mouthed a curse, turned back to him, pointed at the door. "Bottom board, push it in!" She couldn't do more than whisper.

As he pushed in one weatherworn board and crawled through on his knees, she tied back as much of her black hair as was long enough to tie. Two hooks of hair hung down around one eye. When he was through, she crouched and dashed through sideways.

A blade of broken glass gashed her black denim but broke on her flesh.

First floor.

She pushed him on down a long corridor, across the tile, past the derelict diner and the severed pay phones, into the marbled lobby. It sagged now with water damage. The ceiling had a split in it, like a cushion knifed in search of cash. A gray crust crunched underfoot from whatever fluids had gushed once out of that split. Fuzzy loops of decomposing curtains hung like black Spanish moss all over.

He dawdled in the lobby, looking back at the revolving doors they hadn't used, at the half-boarded windows around them, at the shapes gathering at the glass. "What are—?" he began to ask.

"Don't look," she said. She grabbed his clammy hand and pulled him toward the lobby's swooping double staircase, opposite the doors, past a concierge desk that had rotten almost in half.

He still dragged, still looked. A dozen pairs of shining eyes gathered at the windows, heads low to look in under the boards, through the smeared glass. One second they were dog-like faces, short snouts, then they were flat against the pane, no snouts, with swiveling owl heads and solid black beaks cracking the glass.

She pulled him again, got halfway up the staircase before a board snapped, swallowing up half her leg. She lifted it, splinters of miserably rotten wood bending and breaking around her calf, and caught her black boot on the downward-facing spikes of broken wood. "Dammit! Come on!" she said to herself, grabbing her leg around the knee and pulling. The dark denim of her pant leg put out little white tufts of frayed cotton. Splinters broke free of the stairs. She pried her booted foot free. "Son of a bitch," she whispered. Though her pants leg was tattered, her flesh was unharmed. It took more than glass and splinters to break her skin.

She looked at him. He was staring down into the lobby. Shiny black beaks broke through the glass and pried at the boards. Any second now, they'd be in.

"Hey," she said to him, loud.

He looked at her, looked back into the lobby, looked back at her.

"We have to keep moving. Door's up on twelve. We have to keep moving."

He shut his mouth and nodded.

Second floor.

A semicircular walkway looked down on the lobby below. Hallways ran off that ring like spokes, leading to places she didn't know. Between the tops of the twin staircases, in an alcove, was the folding metal gate for the building's elevator. It was an afterthought in a building that never could make up its mind. Hotel? Apartments? Offices? Department store? Different floors answered different questions.

Off the elevator alcove was a door to the building's core, utilitarian stairwell. She pushed it open, pulled him through. He snapped on his bent-necked flashlight and clipped it to his coat. Its white light projected nouveau shapes on the walls, shadows from the stairwell railings.

The stairs were a metal frame running up the inside of a tower of masonry and tile. Broken white tiles lay heaped here at the bottom of the stairwell. The gray bricks visible through the lace-like remains of mortar were like the building's bare flesh.

When she'd come down here after coming into the building—and the city—for the first time, up on the twelfth floor, she'd found this stairwell door blocked from the inside. Someone had jammed a metal desk between the bottom stairs and the door. Entering the stairwell now, she half expected to find this door jammed again. She loved being wrong, sometimes. She exhaled in relief when she saw the metal desk, dragged here from somewhere else in the building, still sitting where she'd left it, under the stairs.

"Help me with this," she said. Together they slid the desk back into place to jam the door. "Should buy us some time." She couldn't bring herself to hope out loud that it would stop them altogether—didn't want to jinx it.

Outside, it sounded like a whole pane of glass hit the lobby floor. Howling, something like a coyote's, mixed with bird-like screeches. They'd be coming up the rotten lobby staircase any second.

"Other doors," he said. "Other stairs?"

She nodded, shrugged. "Don't know. I came down this way. Didn't explore too much. Must be other stairs, but maybe it'll take them time to find them." She looked up the stairwell before them. "A bottleneck like this works in our favor, at least."

Somewhere out there, echoing off the lobby's slashed ceiling, a voice. She couldn't make out the words—they sounded like a record spun slowly backwards—but she felt like they were commands. The screeching turned wholly to baying. She thought of a huntsman driving on hounds, flushing out birds. She didn't want to think it, but she thought it.

"Let's go," she said. They started climbing stairs.

Third floor.

She was faster than him. She didn't like that.

He was younger than she by more than a decade, but he was never spry. He wasn't in bad shape, she knew that for sure, but his breathing went ragged fast. He was pacing himself. She knew that look, when he was pacing himself.

She had longer legs, took the stairs two at a time, and knew how to breathe. She blew the hair away from her eyes as she went.

Fourth floor.

She waited on the landing for him. He wasn't the kind of handsome she used to like, in the other city. He was almost too cute. Too cute to let the Mad City chew him up, she thought.

When he reached the landing, he was breathing fine. She tried to exchange a look with him, but he didn't meet her eyes. She touched his arm. "You still have it?"

He nodded and patted his pea-coat pocket. Still didn't look at her.

"Give it to me," she said.

He looked at her. It felt like he was looking at her forehead. A question slowly materialized on his face.

"Hey," she said. "No time. You go first. I'll keep pace with you. Give me the gun."

He shook his head. "I shoot fine," he said, his voice flat. "Go on. I'm right behind you."

She tilted her head. He had great aim—eerily sharp eyesight—but he was a tentative shooter. What was weird was that he disagreed with her. People changed in the Mad City, sometimes gradually, sometimes suddenly, sometimes into Nightmares, but he seldom disagreed with her. She'd always been convincing, especially to him. "You all right?" she asked.

He nodded yes, then nodded toward the stairs. "No time, right?"

She nodded, slowly, and started up the stairs again. A second later he was moving, too.

Fifth floor.

He was behind her, climbing steps one at a time while she took them two at a time. As they turned on the next landing and headed up the next flight, she saw he kept one hand on the railing, one hand in his pea-coat pocket—the pocket with the gun.

Sixth floor.

He was breathing easy. She looked down at him through the ornate iron railing. He looked back up—past her, it felt like. No nervous smile, no flicker of the eyebrows, none of his anxious habits, which she'd found so cute as recently as that morning.

Seventh floor.

She thought back to that afternoon, to him bleary but looking at her through the steam of black tea in a white Styrofoam cup, when she kissed him and felt him smile. She left him in that street of stalls so she could slip off to the midnight marketplace and trade their scrip for the treasures in her pockets now. She didn't look back, when she left, but now she wished she had.

She slipped her fingers in her pockets again. In one she felt the figurine. In the other, the vial. She kept climbing.

Eighth floor.

They'd wanted to get out of the Mad City together before the city shut tight for that secret hour when its impossible relationship to the slumbering city beyond—or outside, or next door, or above, or below, or whatever it was—kept the Mad City inescapable. For that thirteenth accursed hour, that time in between times, they said the span between the cities was too far to traverse or too solid to pass through or a dozen other things that hardly made sense. She believed them but tonight she thought she'd test the rumors, if it meant getting out before the hounds and their master caught up with them.

If nothing else, she and him would be closer to an exit when the hour was done and ready to make their escape. She kept climbing.

Ninth floor.

She listened to his feet on the iron steps. She thought about what people had said, before, about where the Nightmares came from. "Anyone's a potential Nightmare," she'd heard. "Anyone." She didn't want to think about it. "They hollow you out, or you're hollow already, and they pour something else inside." She thought of the stringy innards of a gourd, all cigarette-ash gray with white seeds.

She looked back at him. He was looking behind him. She didn't want to think about it.

Tenth floor.

Something banged below—something loud. She heard metal whine. The hounds shook the door, shook the desk, shook the stairs. The hinges might give out, down there, or the desk might buckle.

She caught him looking up at her. He seemed calm until he noticed her looking back, then she thought his eyes widened, as if he was just then suddenly afraid. His hand was in his pocket, with the gun.

Eleventh floor.

The top of the stairwell was a mesh of black metal and white glass, smashed and misshapen, like it was a gossamer tent and someone that someone had sat on. Little light came through it.

She looked back. He was slowing. His breathing wavered, just a bit.

"You all right?" she asked.

He smiled, but just his mouth. Only his mouth smiled.

Twelfth floor.

She stepped warily up to the door and tried the handle. It didn't move. "Shit," she said. When she'd been here before, this door had been open, at least from the other side.

"Problem?" he exhaled.

She looked the door up and down for some reason. "Yeah," she said. "Damn thing's locked."

He eyeballed it. "What do we do?" he asked. "They're down there, like, right now."

"Don't I fucking know it." She looked at him. "Give me the gun."

He raised an eyebrow. "Shoot the lock?"

She nodded.

He nodded. "I'll do it." He pulled the gun from his pocket. It was a snub-nosed thing, glinting nickel with a black grip. When he drew it, a handful of bullets fell from his pocket onto the metal landing. Half of them rolled through gaps in the railing and plummeted.

"Dammit," she said, picking the other three fallen rounds off the landing. "How many shots do we have?"

He shrugged, held the pistol in two hands, and took aim at the doorknob. "Six in here, at least." He pulled the trigger and the shot reverberated off the metal door, off the iron and tile, and echoed down the stairwell. The doorknob burst, spun across the landing, and plummeted away.

She stood up, looked at the door, looked at him. As his face became visible through the parting white smoke, he arched his eyebrows. "Be fucking careful with that thing," she said.

He put it back in his pocket. She pocketed the three bullets.

With her fingers, she pried the mechanism in the doorway apart, pulled the bolt back, and yanked the door open. The doorway was stacked, foot to ceiling, with metal desks, bed frames, wooden chairs—anything that might clog the corridor.

"Well, shit," she said, moving her hands in a helpless gesture. She stepped back.

"Clear it?" he asked.

"It'd take forever," she said, looking around. "We should try another floor." She headed down the stairs. A beat later, he was behind her, going down.

Eleventh floor, the door was locked. She kept going.

He started to ask, "Do you want me to shoot—?"

"We'll blow all our ammo on doorknobs," she said, dragging loose hair out of her eyes and dropping onto the next landing.

Tenth floor, door locked. She kept going.

"How far down are you willing to—?" he started. Something downstairs crashed and screeched. The iron stairwell rattled. "Oh, shit."

"Yeah," she said, dropping onto the next landing.

Ninth floor. The door was unlocked.

"Here we go!" she said. "C'mon, c'mon!"

She held the door open for him. He dashed through, the flashlight going with him. The stairwell shook and trembled in the dark to the sound of dozens of heavy feet on it, rushing upward. She heard the baying and the backwards voice bellowing below. She felt her way forward, reached back and pulled the door shut. She found a switch on the knob and turned it.

Up ahead, he turned around, his light shining in her eyes. "Knock it off!" she said.

He turned back around. When her eyes readjusted, she saw they were in some softer part of the building, a place of herringbone carpet and gray wallpaper sewn with silvery floral patterns. She stepped up behind him, relieved at the near-silent swish of her steps on the carpet. Maybe the hounds wouldn't hear which way they'd gone.

Ahead of them, the hallway was dark with long shadows cast by ornate gaslight sconces and glass doorknobs. Nailed-on room numbers cast shadows off each slightly recessed door—919, 918, 917, and on.

"Go on," she whispered in his ear. He looked back over his shoulder at her. He was just shadows and highlights, in the penumbra of his flashlight beam, but when he looked at her, his eyes were bright with a familiar look. She thought he might kiss her. Then it faded.

"Where are we going?" he whispered, moving forward.

"I don't know where the other stairwell is from here," she said. "Or if there even is one, this side of the building."

"So?" He reached a hand behind him, looking for her in the dark. She took it. "The elevator."

He exhaled something like a chuckle. "Little loud—little out of order—don't you think?"

"Yeah," she whispered. "But we're not going to ride it."

As they rounded a corner in what felt like the middle of the hallway's length, she heard the stairwell behind them whine and rattle under the weight of a dozen Nightmares. She hurried him on.

Within a few minutes, they'd forced the folding gate of the elevator shaft's cage open and, satisfied that the car was somewhere below them, she reached out for the frame of the shaft and started climbing upward, this time with feet *and* hands.

"It's just a couple of floors," she whispered.

He made a face. "It's three."

"I'll go first," she offered. "Just try and give me some light."

It was easier climbing than she'd feared. The pattern of metal bars and crossbeams inside the shaft were easy to reach and grip. A faint dose of moonlight fell through another metal-and-glass ceiling at the top of the shaft. Coupled with his flashlight, it was bright enough to thin her fears. She was thankful she couldn't see down any farther.

Somewhere, below the elevator car, the shuffling of something at the bottom of the shaft echoed and pinged off the metal. She wasn't sure what it was—hounds hunting, she assumed—but the car seemed to have it blocked below them. She hoped it couldn't smell them, hoped it couldn't communicate enough to tell others if it heard her and him climbing ten stories above.

Tenth floor.

"The dirtier my hands get," he whispered up to her, "the harder it is for me to keep climbing." The elevator shaft was thick was dust and grime.

Her hands were slipping, too. She shushed him anyway. "Not much longer," she whispered. Then she tossed him a bit of reassurance: "It's easier to see as we get near the top."

Eleventh floor.

His worry made her comfortable. Whatever she had been afraid of before, his fear made her think that he must still be him. She looked down to him and saw him climbing steadily up after her and breathing fine.

A mistake. His flashlight wavered as he climbed and gave her glimpses of the distance to contend with if she slipped—or if he did. Her skin was like stone in the Mad City, she'd felt it turn away knives and she'd felt clubs break on it, but she didn't know what would happen if she fell far enough. Worse, what would happen to him?

"What is it?" he asked.

She blinked. "Sorry," she said and resumed climbing.

Twelfth floor.

With his light on her, she reached back toward the half-open folding gate at the mouth of the twelfth floor and pulled half of it open as far as it would go. The other half wouldn't budge, not from her position. She stepped over, slid through the opening, and nodded down to him.

As he climbed up and through, she listened. She heard the door rattle as he climbed through, heard wind on the glass at the top of the shaft, heard water dripping somewhere… and that was all.

"What is—"

She put her hand over his mouth. His lips felt cold. She shook her head at him, switched off his light, and pulled her hand slowly away. In the dim glow from moonlight above, she indicated for him to follow her.

This was the floor she'd entered on, back when. It was all offices, with frosted-glass foyers and doors, water-damaged tile floors, and a once-white ceiling now sagging from some burst pipe somewhere. She moved down the corridor toward the office where she'd entered, where the strange door that had admitted her hopefully still waited.

Office after office had been meddled with in the intervening time. Someone dragged the furniture in those offices into the hall to choke the corridor and block the stairwell door. She was looking at it now from the other side.

Somewhere on the far side of all that jumbled wood and metal was a stairwell full of Nightmares for all she knew. Ahead of her, just a few paces, was the office door between her and her exit from the Mad City. She stepped up. He followed her.

When she looked back, she saw he had the gun drawn.

She reached the door, put her hand on it, and pushed. It didn't creak, it practically shrieked. Something moved inside the room, something dark and liquid, changing size as it moved from the far wall toward her. She pulled the door shut. As it slammed, he fired.

She spun around. He fired again. He was shooting at the pile of furniture—at oily, suckered tendrils working through the gaps, each one ending in two probing fingers. Something bluish splattered as he fired a third time. Something cried out like an injured dog beyond the debris.

She grabbed him. "Go, go, go!"

They rushed back toward the elevator shaft, broken glass and tile crunching underfoot. He slipped. A tendril grabbed him by an ankle. The fingers became a beak and bit through cloth and flesh. He screamed, fired at the tendril once and missed, fired again and hit home.

She pulled him on to the edge of the elevator shaft. "Can you climb?"

He nodded. He gritted his teeth. His blood was dark, shiny, smeared along the tile behind him where he dragged his limp foot. Something pale was in tatters inside his sock.

"Can you?"

He nodded again.

"Give me it," she said, digging in her pocket for the last three bullets.

He met her eyes. "Yeah," he said. He gave her his gun. She shook out the empty casings and loaded the last three rounds. Furniture crashed to the ground down the corridor.

She leaned into the shaft and fired a shot up at the skylight. One pane fractured and quit and glass fell past her down the shaft. "Okay," she said. "You first."

He shook his head. He kissed her, lots of tongue, no smile this time, and then he shoved her. She almost toppled into the shaft, almost lost the gun, but caught the frame with one hand. "We're almost there," he said.

She glared back at him but he was crowding toward the gate, giving her no choice but to fall or climb. She climbed.

He came after her, trying to hoist himself up with his hands, hopping one foot along the edge of the frame, looking for purchase. She looked up. The pale moon looked like a broken dish, with a curve of porcelain broken off it, like it could cut.

She tucked the gun in her pants. She climbed up and through the empty pane in the skylight, turned herself around on the gravelly roof, and reached down for him. "C'mon!"

As she reached down, tendrils reached up from below, through the half-open gate. He didn't see them but he must've heard the baying that came behind them. He reached up with one hand as a tendril grabbed his wounded leg, wrapping around it like a snake, three coils in one quick move. Another tendril got his other arm. They were so strong that when they pulled him from the wall, he didn't fall. He hung in the grip. He disappeared into it.

She went for the gun, aimed it down the shaft—at nothing but a roiling mass of tendrils hovering, almost, as if moving through water. No sign of him. She fired anyway. She fired both shots. Black goop spattered. She clicked on an empty cylinder. She threw the gun. Then she ran.

Through her eyes, loaded with tears, the roof bobbed and swam around her. She ran over gravel and slate to one edge and then another. Nearby buildings stood half the size as this one. The only fire escapes within reach were a part of this same building, would lead right back down to the nightmares. She looked over her shoulder. Behind her, tendrils slapped down on the roof through the open skylight and fattened into the seamless muscular shapes of bright-eyed black hounds—two, three, four of them.

She put her hands in her pockets. She thumbed the figurine with one hand—some late '80s action-figure hero that he'd lost years ago and wanted for luck back in the other city—but drew out the vial. She popped the rubber stopper out of it with her thumb. She felt it fizz on her finger like soda.

The hounds drew near. She wondered if they would tear her to shreds or try and contain her until their master could arrive. They growled backwards, their insides grinding like gears in a broken engine.

She put the vial to her lips and threw her head back. She downed it all at once and threw the vial off the roof. It filled her stomach, bubbled up her throat, and shook her whole body. Her black-lipped mouth opened, her white teeth shone, and she laughed one quick laugh. Then another. Then she was alive with laughter, eyes wide, hollering, leaning forward like she just got the joke, cackling at the hounds that ringed her. She'd traded a lot of favors, traded tears and tales for that vial, and she'd be damned if she wasn't going to get her taste. She laughed his lost laugh until it ran out. Then she shivered once as it all drained out of her.

She turned, stepped up on the low wall at the edge and ran along that raised edge as far as it went, until the building ran out. There she hurtled herself out into the night, over the alley, toward the next roof, halfway down, to see what damage she could do when her skin hit the city.

The tower rang one time.

WILL HINDMARCH is a writer and designer aiming to write one of everything. Thus far he's been focusing on short fiction, games, scripts, essays, articles, and bloggery. His work has been published in numerous books, magazines, and games. Find him online at *wordstudio.net*.

DON'T HARSH YOUR BUZZ

BY GREG STOLZE

I'M AT A PLACE CALLED "NOW 'N' PERCOLATOR." I've come to rely on coffee. Now 'n' Percolator isn't another upscale latte place with $2.45 scones, it's like the opposite of that. The people who know about it are either really positive—like those scary glaze-eyed tween girls who can't shut up about Twilight—or they'd like to blow the place to Kingdom Come with a hearty block of C-4.

Actually, I only know one guy who wants to blow up coffee shops with C-4 and he thinks the recipe is cream cheese and canned cat-food. He's pretty messed up. People might say the same thing about me. I'm Debra, by the way.

"Debbie?"

Debra. I really prefer Debra these days. I was Debbie to my husband and oh now I've just gotten sad.

"Hi V.S." I give him a smile before I think about it. Recently, when I smile at people, they edge away. I should start covering my mouth, or just wear veils.

V.S. is, according to my best judgment, a really nice, just-plain-decent human being. I'm really worried that he wants to save me.

He sits beside me at the counter and nervously looks right and left. "So are the baristas here any good?" I blink.

"...they make coffee?" I say. The saucer jitters merrily against my cup as I pick it up for a sip. I'm pacing myself.

"Okay." His expression is concerned. "Hey Debbie, how's it been, huh?"

Well. I could tell him the truth, or I could tell him the lie he expects, or I could tell him the lie that would sound like the truth, but instead I blink and then, dammit, I'm somewhere else.

It goes like that.

"Debra."

I smell her before she speaks. It. I smell it. I make a game try of keeping my lip uncurled as I turn. Demonstrating respect is essential.

"Coffee, strong, black!" I call out to the woman behind the counter at Other Drinks, which is several factors weirder than Now 'n' Percolator. It's even more an anti-Starbucks. The directions to take you there would be something like "Get on Highway 53 going south, completely reorient your concepts of spatial causality, and take the exit marked 'Mad City.'"

The counter girl at Other Drinks wears a sleeveless, skintight vinyl dress and a gas mask. When I say 'sleeveless,' I mean it pins her arms to her sides, leaving her hands to emerge from holes down by her hips. They look like vestigial fish fins. All her cups and bottles and shakers are at waist level so she can shuffle about preparing beverages at pubis-height. The dress looks so vacuum-formed that her ankles are pressed together, constricted. She never speaks, and she's barefoot on the dirt floor as she wobbles here and there, filling the filter, taking for-freaking-ever about it. Eventually, I have to steel myself, look away from her, and turn to Sue with a smile.

"Sue!" I say and I know it sounds totally false, but Sue may not be able to tell. I don't know exactly what Sue is, or the other things like her. Like it.

We call them 'Nightmares,' but that's just the cover we throw over our ignorance. We call them that when we aren't just screaming, or dying. We usually die around them, but this one wants something.

Sue Wedgeflow is a Nightmare and she looks like a really pretty black woman, belly-dancer body and fat brown dreadlocks, glossy like her face, hair the same tone as her skin, a little too shiny, like her skin is wet and like her dreads are too, her clothes are all the same brown tone and so are the sclera of her eyes and her perfectly aligned teeth. She looks like she was made from wet clay, an unfired Ethiopian Galatia, until you catch the scent and think, no, that's not clay.

Nightmares are racist, did you know? Not that they espouse racist ideology as much as they embody the forbidden, suppressed, disgusting and inchoate baggage people carry. Or something. I don't know. I hate Sue for looking black on behalf of every black human I've ever known, even though I'm not black, because she's not human.

"Debra. How are you?"

"Human."

"Of course." Her brown smile gets a little hungry. "Always always always."

The black-sheathed barista totters over, her ship's prow bosom right at eye level as she sets my coffee in front of me, gas-mask valve between her clavicles like an Egyptian king's beard. How the hell does she go to the bathroom in that getup? Is it some kind of... sex thing?

She has to get permission from her master to get out of the bondage and drop a tinkle? I don't get it.

I'm drifting again. Sue Wedgeflow wants me to betray all of mankind and I'm considering it. I pick up the coffee and inhale deeply through my nose to cut her stench. Its stench.

"Hm?" I'm back at Now 'n' Percolator, and the smell of coffee grounds, patchouli oil and time-killing transients blends nicely with the aroma coming off V.S., which is like a fresh-sharpened pencil. I lean towards him to sniff, then disguise it by appreciatively smelling this coffee cup, which is a chipped white porcelain number printed with ads for local businesses. (In Other Drinks, it was a tiny demitasse carved from a single flawless emerald or something. I wasn't really paying attention.)

"How are you, Debbie?"

"Debra," I say without thinking, then look away to add a sugar and stir, though I usually take it black. "I'm… going by 'Debra' now."

"I haven't seen you at church," he says. "You switch to the later service?"

"Um, I… not…"

"Sorry, I'm being pushy." Now it's his turn to look down in his cup and pretend it's absorbing all his attention.

We're Lutherans, me and V.S. or, anyhow, I was a Lutheran. I haven't been back since the funeral. Big-ass funeral, three for the price of one. Cindy, Nadia and Mark and you know how when you wake up from oversleeping and your mouth feels gummy and gross? I feel like everything from my heart to my uterus has been like that since. Not that I've overslept much.

"You're not," I say. "You aren't. I appreciate it. I've been having a… hard time."

He turns his cup in a circle on the mismatched saucer. The guy behind the counter is the source for the patchouli smell. He has those horrid ear-stretcher rings and a beautiful smile breaks through his haystack beard when a girl with blonde cornrows walks in. There's a college nearby. Cindy was about that age.

"I remember," V.S. says softly, "when my mom died? I mean, she'd been sick a long time and so it wasn't sudden, not…" He coughs, covers it with a sip. "Right after, everyone was so nice and supportive and helpful and, like, the hams and soups…"

"Everyone brings a hot dish," I say, with a little smile but a real one.

"But too soon, way too soon, they want everything to be normal. You go back to work and it's like, 'Are you still on about that? It was weeks and weeks ago!'"

"And at home," I say, "you're still getting used to not hearing his ringtone on your phone or finding his coffee offerings…"

"Coffee offerings?" V.S. asks. He was more Mark's friend than mine. They were the choir's baritone section and talked about football.

"Mark was constantly making coffee and then leaving the cup sitting out, half-finished. I'd find them in the bedroom, the microwave, the table by the sofa… I said they reminded me of people leaving offerings for their household gods in China or, like, wherever…"

For a minute we're quiet and it's all right.

"How's work?" V.S. asks quietly.

"I've… taken… a sabbatical." I lie, and it's not as easy as most lies because I'm not used to misleading normal people. I've gotten good at redirecting insomniac lunatics, but V.S. is nice and I worry that the techniques are different.

He nods, though, so either it's easier on healthy people (healthy mentally) or he's just not calling me on my B.S.

"So if you aren't going to work, what are you doing?"

"Drinking a lot of coffee!" I say brightly. "Speaking of which will you excuse me I have to go to the bathroom?"

The unisex toilet in the Now 'n' Percolator is pretty grim but the bathroom in Other Drinks is just a chipped porcelain pot on the dirt floor with a brass bell on a rope next to it, labeled "Ring When Full." On the floor beside it is a manhole with a metal disc cover. Luckily I finish before I realize I can hear breathing from underneath it.

"See, I love that!" Sue says when I return, blinking stickily and smiling. "Biological function is so intricate and inevitable and I want that. I want that from you."

"Yeah," I say. "See, I've been thinking that maybe I don't want... to..."

"Want to what? 'Come to the Dark Side'?" Her tone is jovial and if she didn't stink like a hot, rainy garbage strike it would be easy to chuckle along. "We're not your enemies, Debra. We just don't understand."

"You've killed a lot of people," I murmur. I can't look her in the eye.

"Me personally? Or my kind?"

"Both?"

"I've only killed fifteen human beings," she says, and she sounds really proud. "For as long as I've been around, that's a very small number!"

"Yay you," I mutter into my drink, taking another rationed sip.

"It's not necessary," she says. "You could become a Nightmare and not kill anyone at all ever!"

I mistrust her enthusiasm.

"Look, I appreciate all you've done for me," I say, though mostly that consists of non-murder. "But I like humanity, y'know? It's a personal thing. It fits my tastes." I'm babbling and she knows it.

"Do you? Like humanity?"

"Oh yeah!"

"Because it's complicated and intricate and pulls you in a dozen directions at once?" Her teeth glint as she leans in. "Because that's what I want, Debra. Reality is a very real thing, all evidence to the contrary aside."

"Um..."

"Being more real than you, we have to be pure," she says, voice earnest. "We have to be one thing. Tacks with his order, and Tock with his punishment, forever and ever amen, and they want to wear the edges off your inefficiencies until you fit. But humans won't. Won't won't won't! You won't fit and won't sit still and won't be a tidy, labeled category. I love that!" I think she wants to grab my hands. I will scream if she does, there's no way I couldn't. Even with her face hidden and her posture constrained, the girl in vinyl looks embarrassed somehow and is hop-stumbling to the far end of the counter.

"You never stopped being a mommy," Sue says, a jealous accusation. "Even when you had to! You never stopped being little Mark's little wifey-wife even though he's dead but it says right there, in the, the thing, it says 'until death do us part' and you're breaking the rules. Why won't you let me? Why can't I break the rules too?"

"Well," I say, trying not to lean back, "There's only so much humanity to go around. It's a, what, a hot commodity?"

"But that's why we're so perfect for each other!" she cries. "You get to give up on humanity and see what's beyond it! I can't explain what matters to you Debra, but you can know! You've done it all," she says, petulant. "Love and sorrow and tedium and comfortable suburban hypocrisy oh god when's it my turn?"

She could flat murder me in a heartbeat. I know this. She's a Nightmare after all and me? I'm just frail flesh, an emergent system of survival integrating heartbeat and lung-swell and nerve-jolt, mediated by caffeine and emotion. She's pure idea. Who could withstand?

"If I… do," I say, "What will I turn into?"

"Up to you," she purrs. "You've had all the practice anyone could expect inventing a personality, you the living do it every time you enter a new social clique. But this time you could be firm, fixed and forever and wouldn't that make a nice change? You could rest."

"I won't be with them," I say, and it's not a question or an answer or anything.

"You have a limited human perspective, from which the relationship described by 'with them' just does not make sense."

"What's death?" I ask her, turning to her and I'm inches from that horrid shit face because for just a moment I'm brave or maybe don't care. "What is death?"

"You know as well as any human." She's all coy and confident, all of a sudden and she says we're the changeable ones?

"We just snuff out," I say. "That's it, isn't it? We're here, then we're gone."

"Do not," she replies, "fall back on the comfortable lie of human insignificance. We're more real than you and all we do is embody your ideas, your symbols, your class consciousnesses and social divisions. So I'm sorry Debra no, you can't just hide your head under the warm fuzzy nihilism blanket. You matter. Every last one of you petty pretty primitives matters."

"So you want to be one."

"More than anything, and you're the only one who can give it to me. Miss Back-and-Forth, you're the swinging door and I am ready to swing!"

"I…" I blink. "I need to think about this."

"Then think. But don't take too long."

V.S. looks like he's trying to occupy the minimum volume of space with his body, while Bush-Beard the counter-man flirts with his blonde friend.

"Debbie," he starts, then corrects himself. "Debra."

"That coffee goes right through me!"

"I'm really worried."

"About what?" Sure, that's going to fool the hell out of him.

He gives me a flat, 'don't get cute' look. "About you."

"Oh V.S., that's sweet but I'm… I'm really…" I can't do it! I can't say 'fine!'

"I went by your house," he says, voice low. "When was the last time you were back there?"

"Um…" It was when Illy Billy and Deirdre got killed, and Stan the Can Man went insane, but I don't think I should say that.

"You've got mail piling up in the mailbox, overflowing," V.S. continues. "Where have you been sleeping?"

"Nowhere," I whisper. Then, louder, "Look, it's not a problem, you don't have to, um, concern yourself..." Coffee. I drink some coffee. Is there anything it can't fix? Need to stay awake, work harder, avoid symbol-parasitizing reality collapses or just pause while lying to a compassionate human being who wants to help you? Coffee gets it done!

"Why don't you come stay with me and Evonne for a while?" he says gently, and puts his hand on my hand.

"I AM NOT GOING TO SLEEP AT YOUR HOUSE!" I scream and all the hipsters and homeless and college-age poetesses spin and stare. Some immediately look back into their drinks, as embarrassed as the shrink-wrapped drink-slave, while others glare at V.S., who turns bright crimson. But he doesn't get up and scuttle away, he holds my hand tighter and says, "I think you should come with me right now."

"...now?" I whimper and I know I'm back at Other Drinks. Even though I didn't hear anything said I know I've used up Sue's patience.

"Your choice is very simple," she says. "Or, it would be if you weren't a human being and weren't bound and determined to make every obvious thing into an elaborate moral debate full of pitfalls and hidden issues. You can transcend the tangled mess of human existence, all that pain and uncertainty and grief and selfishness, you can become more real, a fixed point in relation to the betrayal and deception and misunderstanding endemic to the human condition. You can go through one last change and put a period at the end instead of your endless, bottomless, pointless question marks. Or you can chicken out, clutch your dead feelings for your dead family to a heart that has no further purpose. You can run, and drink coffee, and squirm, until you die. Because you'll die, Debra. And I swear by all that's teleological, if you make the change you won't even care, it's your stupid human prejudices that make you want to keep breathing at any cost! Your only long-term survival chance, though… even if you get past me… even if Tacks and Tock don't mutilate you once I withdraw my protection… even if you get rested and get medicated and get lied to until you rejoin the shuffling ignorant masses… that buys you, at best, seventy years? Seventy bleak years of failing health and loneliness and decay, getting saggy and wrinkled and senile, losing everything but the perfect memory of Mark, of Cindy at her most beautiful, of…"

"No you're wrong." Sue does not look happy when I interrupt, and I have to giggle. "You're so silly, I'm already losing them. I can't remember what Mark's morning breath smelled like, or how the comb tugged in my hands when I caught it in Nadia's hair. I know those things, but they're not real memories any more. Someday, the first-degree memories will all go and I'll just have their shadows."

"Then what's holding you back?"

"I'm pretty uneasy with the idea of unleashing you, in a human body, on the waking world."

"Me?" Her surprise looks perfect, genuine. "I'd be harmless! I'm far more dangerous now than bound in some farting, failing, aging anatomy! I'd be confused and disoriented, misled and lied-to and plagued by imperfect comprehension," she says, voice thick with longing, "And I'd get old, and I'd die! I'd get to die Debra, and if you don't do this for me, then do it for humanity! You hate us and we hurt you and you can save all my future victims, I lied about the fifteen, it's hundreds! It's thousands, I killed thousands! Millions maybe! Illy Billy and Deirdre weren't the last, just the most recent, they'll be the middle point of a vast succession unless you trade with me!" She's panting, and I can see wet lines on those lovely cheekbones. So either she's weeping, or she understands enough to fake tears, or it's just some coincidental... oozing.

If I'd already taken the bargain, I wouldn't be wondering. I'd be so pure, such a creature of fixed idea that, right or wrong, I could only have one opinion. Their utter self-certainty is what makes the Nightmares so dangerous and, at the same damn time, the only thing that lets us get away with anything. And right now, being certain about anything sounds awful tempting.

"If you won't do it for me, or for yourself, do it for mankind," she whimpers, and it sounds lame, stupid, as fake as a line from a movie, quoted by a teenage boy trying to get laid.

"What would I have to do?" I ask.

"Just put your head down," she says, hope firing her eyes. "When you wake up..."

"...everything will look a lot different."

V.S. called ahead—how do I know this? Evonne made up the guest bed and it's the most beautiful thing I've ever seen, so cool and flat and it smells like daylight, not like fabric-softener perfume but like cloth stretched on a clothesline until the sun's UV rays have washed out all the bacteria and microscopic skin flakes and ah god I'm filthy but I want to lie on those fresh sheets so bad, I want to lie down and give in.

"There's nothing wrong with you that rest and a shower won't fix," V.S. says from the doorway as Evonne helps me sit on the edge, kick off my shoes, take off my crusty old sweater and I'm going to mess up this perfect bed, it's clean and I'm dirty.

"No I can't I mustn't," I mumble but Evonne just tucks me in like I'm a little girl again, like when I was little with a fever and everything got unreal and frightening.

I say "Don't let me…" even as she leans in and says "Go to…" and our words blend as my head hits the softest pillow in history.

"…sleep."

When he's not designing RPGs both indie and mainstream, **GREG STOLZE** has foolishly chosen to write across a sprawling range of tones and topics, ranging from the quirky magical realism of *Switchflipped* and the gritty Mythos-meets-military novel *Mask of the Other* through literary realism, historical horror and wistful science fiction. You can get a taste of all the above at *http://www.gregstolze.com/fiction_library/*. Also, he folds origami.

DON'T LOSE YOUR SHIT

BY ROBIN D. LAWS

Neil Worrell serves as reviewer-without-portfolio for PostMusic.com and is a regular contributor to the Earworm Podcast. ShiftGauge named Neil one of 2010's Music Thinkers To Watch, while Band Or Album? frontman Chris Musser called him "a pestilential maggot turd in the outhouse of journalism." *Magnet Pulls and Ketchup Spills*, his critical discography of Tortoise, will be published in 2013 by Backbeat Press.

EVER SINCE ROCK CRITIC NEIL WORRELL learned the secret of not going to sleep anymore he's spontaneously invented a new invisible punctuation mark

Which is why he's headed into this convenience store

Because he does not want to lose his grasp of the invisible perception mark

No, punctuation mark punctuation mark

Punctuation mark that exists suspended halfway between period and comma

Just as Worrell is suspended between sleep and waking

Has entered an entire new dimension of perception and power

So maybe it is a perception mark as well as a punctuation mark absolutely absolutely it is

But he does not want to lose the thread of it

As he is losing the thread of so much else

The lyrical spasms of the latest self-titled Potato Man record invest us in a new realm of

shit shit no lost it

The lyrical spasms of the new Potato Man record invest us in a new realm of

no nope it's gone

Gone Like a Train Bill Frisell Lefty Frizzell post-rock's debt to mountain music he's going into this convenience store because of its freakishly wide selection of energy drinks which are required to maintain the state of awakefulness required to catch hold of the thread of the punctuation mark the perception mark

because of its freakishly wide selection of energy drinks and its clientele

who he senses know something of his condition

perhaps share his condition or did so in the past

but for whatever reason he can't crack through to them

can't get them to spill

Built To Spill disproves an axiom of John Cage's of John Cale's of Papa John Phillips of Papa John's Pizza

That's the punctuation mark the perception mark right there the sentences never stop they just loop around fork around run in parallel he's thinking in seven directions in once and that's why you need the perception mark to punctuate them, the punctuation mark to perceive them

Ever since he abandoned sleep

Sleep abandoned him

Sleep never existed this is the true world what with the real city underlying this one

underlying all other cities

the one that connects all those who see the perception marks

what with its tick-tick-ticking cops its office supply store headed hydra soulsuckers the origami gangstas the gut tunnels that horrible place where kids are trapped

(like Neil was, as a kid, in the infinite blandfield of the twin cities suburban middle school high school dreamcrushing machinery eternal boredom containing the mind for the job pool to extinguish the dissent of individuality)

except there's no city to escape to

because **this is the city**

and places worse that Worrell has yet to venture

 until he figures out more of what's going on

which means getting these mooks, these eternal convenience store denizens who

Convenience store: a place where you buy convenience

just as the latest Beyoncé opus encourages you to purchase a de-deracinated and thus defanged bourgeois aspiration

see also Oprah as the rags to riches goddess of late
capitalism

all hip hop artists since Arrested Development's
Unplugged as consumerism's mayflies

which means getting these guys who habitually habituate perceptually punctuate the Ready Mart at Hazel and Fifth down by the industrial zone

a zone where no one should need to purchase convenience because everyone who comes here has by definition gone out of their way

to be where no one needs to be

no one except maybe the overall-wearing uniformed legions (ballcapped/hard-hatted) who arrive in their big rigs their mud-yellow construction vehicles driving them behind the chainlink fences to the steel and concrete structures beyond

what with their domes and towers and gantries

that mysterious land

Part of the waking/sleeping false city, or part of the Real City only Worrell can see

Only Worrell and a bunch of others

A bunch of others including he suspects the convenience store lurkers forever passing the giant fridge, the wall-sized fridge, moving past it like swimming sharks anticipating chum

Their eyes on the energy drinks contained within

The familiar brands: Red Bull, Rock Star, Monster, No Fear, the little red-capped bottles by the counter

At the counter

(by the way)

Where there would normally be rows of gum, of mints, of cough drops and throat lozenges and sweet-flavored relievers of gastrointestinal distress

Instead it's all caffeine pills

But Worrell already understands that the caffeine pills don't do it the caffeine pills are for rubes tyros wannabes

a test to ensnare the unwary, a mechanism filtering the seers from the seen

the be-ers from the been

One caffeine pill over the line and you reverse course the body crashes the brain relaxes you surrender to sleep and the super powers and the heightened consciousness

The caffeine pills are not where it's at: the initiated go for the energy drinks

Worrell fades behind the corner of an endcap puffed with potato chip bags contents may have settled during shipping all product sold by weight

And he watches

He studies the denizens, the probable other awakers, as they patrol the aisles, slowing noticeably as they pass the energy drinks, glancing furtive

Real beads of sweat on their foreheads matching the illustrated beads of condensation printed on the aluminum tins of the drink cans

Worrell clocks their gazes, follows the micro-shifts of their eye movements notes the flickers and flashes toward individual cans

Some cans dosed with numinous power, others ordinary

containing only the standard concoction of guarana and sugar and vitamins and taurine and carnitine so the trick is figuring out which are the jackpot cans and which are the jackhole cans

Drink a jackpot and you're going up levels and unlocking achievements and Mick Jagger up up up

Down a jackhole and you're crashing and burning and buggering your save points and Sid Vicious spiraling out Elliott Smith diving on a steak-knife Mark Linkous shot to the heart except you don't die you wake up

which is worse

Worrell clocks their vibes, the swimming sharks, the fiends for wakefulness, twitching, sweating, eager for a jackpot, terrified of a jackhole

Where Worrell only intuits the rules these fuckos **know** them

Know as the oppressed know the contours of the jackboot

To learn the the intricacies of the trifecta, of the tote bets in all their variety, seek the degenerate gambler

To learn the odds of the Great Drink Fridge, swim with the punksharks

Worrell clocks their faces mentally he calls them either Mister or Missus something

There's Mister Wrinkly, creased face, rumpled pants, buzzcut, nicotine teeth, scarecrow bones

Mister Tapeglasses young sandy hair pimples big-assed truck tire tattoo on flabby upper arm

Missus Housewife fuzzy blue slippers fuzzy pink bathrobe T-shirt with photorealistic poodle design peroxide damaged stringy hair

Missus Political line of buttons pinned to her army surplus bag each bearing a lefty slogan, flopping brown hair up in clips black top multicolored peasant skirt

Mister Tall who Worrell originally designated Mister Blackguy but then caught himself being racist and so now focuses on his height but he is bald and hands callused and wears a tight red T and khaki work pants but when you get right down to it his distinguishing feature from the others is that they are all white and that makes him the black guy

Neil Worrell works for effectively less than minimum wage at his friend's used vinyl store while writing for a bunch of stupid music blogs. He eats ramen three nights a week. By the time he finishes his involuted nerd-out over a post-rock band the publisher will likely be out of business. His last sexual encounter took place two years ago and consisted of humiliating ex-sex.

Worrell clocks them

They all clock the energy beverages

Seriously the case, unit after unit, door after door, contains only energy drinks where in another store there would be a few shelves of energy drinks and then one unit of milk, two of pop, there'd be eggs and lunch meat and yogurt and whatever the hell else hot dogs maybe

This has to be the ground zero of awakers then

And what the punksharks are clocking are the offbrands the mystery brands the varieties of energy drink Worrell has seen nowhere else

And no question about it lately Worrell has been looking

At no other retail location has he found Thoughtbomber, Springheel Jack, Whoaboy or Headbump.

Cap'n Thud emblazoning the cartoon smile of a Caribbean pirate, crazy eye-swirls beneath beetling brow

Decay Rate wrapped in a lenticular sleeve swirling with optical illusion

Filipino Uncle with its leering man in a tropical shirt, daring you to sup of his decapitated pineapple

Dozens of cans of WSB in either freshmint or cowboy or original flavor with the fedora and glasses and dour face of William S Burroughs pistol in hand ready to shoot another something off his wife's head

I mean the rest might be obscure brands but that last is a sure sign that reality has shifted here

that this is a special place in the not entirely positive way all greatness arises from

If it was just a matter of picking one of the crazy brands the punk-sharks would have grabbed their cans and been long gone but they're cruising cruising so even with those

Maybe with the crazy brands there's a higher hit rate

But even with those you're not sure of a jackpot or immune from a jackhole

Not all awakers come here so maybe there's a level you reach where you don't need this anymore or other routes or whatever but Worrell can feel sleep tugging at him and he's sure that if he jackholes now he's not only going to lose it all

the superpowers etcetera

but also long-term health repercussions arrythmic heartbeat

Chronic fatigue

Permanent talent loss

He can't afford a jackhole now has to figure the rules, outfigure the punksharks, mainline his way to undying residence in the True City, terrors and all

Start with stealth

Mess them up if needed

But start with stealth so Worrell watches them

Mister Tapeglasses makes a break for it speeds up

The others swept up behind him increase their pace too

Tapeglasses swerves for the brass-colored handle of fridge door number three

The others bunch up close behind him

He opens the door

They stop

Holding their breath

Worrell holding his breath

Tapeglasses loses his nerve

Deflates

Moves on

Worrell guesses he was going to reach for a cerulean blue can of Slave Dagger

Maybe it's jackhole and Tapeglasses sensed it last minute

Maybe it's jackpot and Tapeglasses simply got the fear

Worrell perceives the flaw in the follow the punksharks' plan

They're punksharks

By definition

Even if they've got the lore

They're too punk to act on it

Because the stakes are too high

Worrell could bet on Tapeglasses losing the gut check

Grab the Slave Dagger

Blast it down

But if it sleeps him then that's it

It's madness that's what it is

Maddening madness

Neil Worrell hasn't slept for what he thinks is a two-week period but might be any subjectively telescoped or elongated period of time. During a dark period last year he had vivid thoughts about rape but never acted on them. Something is moving around inside him, something cartilaginous.

An electronic two-tone chime announces the arrival in the store of a dark coated fedora hatted figure his face wide his torso triumphantly fat

In biker boots he makes blowhard strides to the big fridge sideburns waggling sunglasses gleaming

(It's night by the way)

Biker Boots grabs the handle to door number three

Yanks it open

Grabs the can

The exact can

Of Slave Dagger Regular Mister Tapeglasses had been circling

Yells out to Counter Guy *Hey I'm popping an **Ess-Dee*** emphasis on the first syllable.

Counter Guy yells back *You're good for it Dix*

Mister Tapeglasses shrinks implodes dies inside

Contents hiss as Dix aka Biker Boots pulls the tab

Glugs it down

Wipes his face

Grins at Tapeglasses

As if to say *sucker*

And strut-stomps to the counter

Slapping down his single plus coins

Presumably exact change

Seeya he says

Feelya says Counter Guy

Who at this point takes note of Worrell as if for the first time

(This is the longest Worrell has spent in the store

always by instinct avoiding Counter Guy's gaze)

Counter Guy seeming like he stepped out of 1961

short sleeve dress shirt brown slacks belt

face narrow and hawkish

Counter Guy calls down to Worrell *Can I help you*

No just looking says Worrell

Annoyed because now the punksharks are muttering amongst themselves about what just happened

that's what Worrell wants to be eavesdropping on

not justifying himself to the clerk

Shoulda gone for it says Missus Housewife

Dix didn't get jackholed says Missus Political

Don't make it worse says Tapeglasses

Mister Tall wags a finger *when you sense it you just gotta gusto it*

Tapeglasses pouts *easy for you to say*

Tall throws up beefy hands *Whatever man whatever*

Tapeglasses goes defensive *When was the last time you went for it seriously huh you're about to snooze you can't even manifest that levitation stunt no more mojo draining from you by the minute I'll be surprised you come back tomorrow or ever*

Fuck you Horton says Tapeglasses

Fuck you right back says Tall

Mister Tall opens door number two

Grabs a mini of Minnesota Beater pops it open drinks it down

Hey you gonna pay for that Counter Guy yells

Give us a break here Missus Political answers back

Mister Tall turns gray looks bad

Goes from sweaty to drenched

Oh no he says

Staggers into the toiletries aisle

Knees buckling

Falls to the tile floor

Worrell the only one dares to look at him

Not any of the punksharks

Not Counter Guy even

Mister Tall snores

Eyes REMMING wild under his lids

To the others it's like he's not there like he vanished from sight like they can't allow themselves to write him into their reality

The rest of the punksharks resume their circuit past the fridge and around

Worrell finds himself falling in line with them

Replacing Mister Tall in their ecosystem

They nod at him sad-eyed

Brothers and sisters in the brothersisterhood of punks

Too needful of jackpot too fearful of jackhole

Hey

Worrell starts

Counter Guy has snuck up behind him

Put a hand on his shoulder

Violating his precious personal space

You better get going says Counter Guy

I'm just looking Worrell twitches

Been here an awful long time for just looking

I got a right to be here

Actually you don't

Please I just need to stay awake

Maybe you ought to do it somewheres else

Worrell goes small *Please let me stay*

Believe me this place ain't for you

Then explain it to me

Counter Guy gives Worrell his back

walks away

heading to the register

Some balls on you Mister Wrinkly says

Missus Housewife shakes her head disapproving *Asking Counter Guy to explain*

Then you explain Worrell hears himself saying

We don't know you

We don't need you here

Go find your own Big Fridge

There are other Big Fridges Worrell asks

they look at him like he's an idiot

Worrell grabs Tapeglasses

Hey let go asshole

The sleeping guy you said he used to be able to levitate what can you do

I said let me go

Missus Political starts hollering for the Counter Guy Worrell loses his shit he whirls on her and grabs her *you wanna be in this I'll put you in this*

A hole in Worrell's chest cavity inches below his right clavicle opens up and a cartilaginous member chest-bursters out of it blood blood bone blood the cartilaginous member wraps itself around Missus Political's neck *tell me tell me tell me* Worrell is screaming she's talking they're all talking but Worrell can't hear them now above the din of the cartilaginous member shrieking in his ear demanding its due

It's all going wrong

yes, he's losing his shit

Counter Guy is there

The others all yield to him

Worrell talks in the cartilaginous member's voice demanding answers an apology and a surefire jackpot can

Counter Guy's arm is a shotgun now

Let her go pal this is your last warning

Worrell's cartilaginous member pulls Missus Political closer *I will let her go but you gotta tell me you gotta explain what the hell's going on here all I know is I gotta stay awake I gotta maintain my power gotta keep this thing fed and what it eats is me not sleeping so you have to tell me how this works how to distinguish jackpot from jackhole*

Let her go **NOW** the shotgun arm pumping a round into its chamber KA-CHUNK

There's got to be a way that Dix guy could tell he got a jackpot I need to know I don't mean to hurt any of you but I'm telling you I need to understand

Cartilaginous member tightens around Missus Political's neck hard appendages sprouting from it digging into her flesh drawing blood spurting spurting

Counter Guy jerks his arm which is the trigger pulling action and the round BOOMS out and Worrell goes down and

Part of **Neil Worrell's** head is missing

Last thing Worrell hears is Mister Tall snoring
Period.

The fiction of author and game designer **ROBIN D. LAWS** includes *The Rough and the Smooth*, *The Worldwound Gambit* and the upcoming *Blood of the City* and *New Tales of the Yellow Sign*. Robin created the GUMSHOE investigative roleplaying rules system and such games as *Feng Shui*, *The Dying Earth*, *The Esoterrorists* and *Ashen Stars*. Find his blog, a cavalcade of film, culture, games, narrative structure and gun-toting avians, at *robindlaws.com.*

DON'T BLEACH YOUR MEMORIES

BY MUR LAFFERTY

SERGEANT PATRICK FOGARTY LOOKED AT THE BLOOD that still dripped from the ceiling, the chunks of flesh discarded on the floor, and the sculpture of organs and intestines on the dining room table. The first officer on the scene was still outside, cleaning the sick off his shoes. Sergeant Fogarty hadn't vomited; he had seen worse. Although he couldn't remember when.

The mother of the chunks of flesh had gone catatonic with shock, and who could blame her? This would be an easy case, though, as the sick fuck had stayed behind to feast on his project, while naked, and the mother had brained him with a Stephen King book before he could get up. He was out cold, locked in the back of the squad car. Fogarty assumed they'd have to take him to the hospital or something. At the very least they should pump his stomach.

The mess was legendary. The coroner would be there to collect as much as she could, but that would still leave the blood soaked into the carpet and the stains on the ceiling as a reminder to the mother—if she ever came out of her catatonic state. Fogarty knew there were several crews who claimed they could clean a mess like this, but this one called for the big guns.

He pulled out his wallet and fingered the business card. He didn't like calling the number on the card, but when he needed a big job done, this was the guy to do it, and do it well. Fogarty just had to ignore the fact that the guy was so damn creepy... he sighed and dialed the number on his cell.

Eloin Gomez arrived half an hour later in his black, unmarked van. He nodded once to the officer at the door, who let him in. He was a tall man, dressed in an Italian suit with a peculiar cut; Fogarty always wondered if he'd had them custom made. A scarlet handkerchief was in his breast pocket, looking like a splash of blood. His hair was cropped short, and his goatee was trimmed, and he looked as if he belonged in a penthouse office, not cleaning shit and blood from a murder scene. But his eyes were not those of a man of business. They were a little too wide, with deep purple circles underneath, like he had seen too much.

Gomez shook Fogarty's hand, making eye contact. Fogarty fought the desire to look away.

"Sergeant. What do we have here?"

"Some sick asshole cut up a kid, played with the insides, and then started eating. We got the guy, and the mom is in shock right now, but we've got a serious shithole of a mess."

Gomez nodded. "May I see the room?"

Fogarty motioned for him to follow. "Yeah, Doctor Baldur ought to be done by now."

The coroner, a small, mousy woman with startlingly long eye lashes nodded to Fogarty as she left the dining room, holding several stacked plastic containers in her hands. After a flick of her eyes to take in Gomez, she didn't look at him again.

The cleaner did not flinch when he saw the dining room. It looked slightly better with the flesh and organs removed, but the blood was still drying on the walls and ceiling, and more bodily fluids coated the floor and tabletop. The smell, coppery blood and foul shit and that special odor of spilled viscera, was nearly overpowering. Fogarty held his sleeve over his nose and fought to control his stomach.

Gomez made no attempt to cover his nose, but walked slowly around the room, peering closely at different blood stains. Once, his long nose nearly touched the wall as he studied a stain. He winced at one point, and his hand came up to touch briefly the handkerchief in his pocket.

He stepped around the blood pools, but apparently didn't care when his expensive shoes met with the tacky fluid. He touched the blood on the wall once, muttering to himself, and reached a long finger out to touch the stuff.

"How many children were in the house?"

"One body was here," Fogarty replied.

"No, there is another child's blood here. The boy's is on the floor and table, but another—a girl—contributed the spray on the ceiling and walls. She is very likely dead, but you will probably want to find the body."

"Another kid? Are you sure?"

"I'm always sure. Come test the DNA if you like. But—" he dragged his finger through the blood, "you will likely find the body in the garage freezer. Perhaps the killer wanted to save it for later."

Fogarty ran for the garage. He hated how Gomez knew things, how he was always right.

Gomez shook his head as the portly sergeant exited the room. He'd known the girl was there the moment he'd seen the room. Every stain, every different fluid, had a story. There was once a time when he couldn't tell if a blood-covered wall came from one person or twenty, but that was months ago. Now they spoke to him, individual stains with individual stories, the boy's voice louder than the girl's. But that was simply because there was more of him.

Gomez began making a list of what he would need for a proper cleaning. The fear that the stains conveyed was palpable; interestingly enough, red hot hatred came from the boy, too. These would be good enough for trade. Surprise and fear from the girl would be useful too. And of course, pain from both. It radiated from the stains in waves.

Gomez touched the handkerchief in his pocket again, thinking of the stain on it that radiated all the time, that would never let him forget her.

He no longer loves me. No more. No longer. No.

Usually, Gomez would wait for the police to leave before he got started. They were suspicious of him enough, they didn't need to see his methods. However, he'd seen a door in the backyard of a neighboring house, and he wanted to grab the convenience while it was there. Some nights he wasted hours looking for a way in.

From the inside pocket of his expensive suit he brought out two tiny crystal vials. He held one vial in front of his mouth and leaned in close, and listened.

It's mister Marsh marshface marsh mash marsh fart I hate him he sent me to detention and then he made me do the things I hate the things I hate him I hate him I hate him oh no not Jenny why is she here Jenny no study group Jenny go home go home please please no so much blood now me now my turn I don't want—

As the words came into his head from the stains, he let them flow through his head, past his lips, and into the vial until it glowed a burnt orange.

He repeated the process with the girl's blood. Hers was a much shorter, much more surprised taste, but still strong enough, Gomez figured.

Why is Mr. Marsh here why he's got a knife he's mad at Tony mad mad mad why Tony? Why me? Run run run run oh mommy the PAIN—

Like police officers and doctors, Gomez had hardened himself to the pain of human suffering, or else he would break down each day on the job. But the cases with kids were the worst.

Well. Almost the worst.

Eloin doesn't love me anymore. Why did you say those things, Eloin? I love you—

Gomez was stowing the vials in his pocket when Fogarty came back in. "You were right. How the fuck you know this is beyond me. I'd think you were an accomplice except that you are right on all of them." He gave Gomez a hard look, and Gomez smiled his tired smile and bowed.

"I am here to serve. I have what I need; I will be back around midnight and the place will be clean by morning."

"You going to ask your usual crackpot bullshit price?" Fogarty asked, raising an eyebrow.

Gomez paused. "I'd think you would be grateful I do not drain the city's coffers."

"Whatever. What will you need this time?"

Gomez pretended to think, but he already knew. "I will require a toy of the boy's, preferably a stuffed animal of some sort, and a lock of the girl's hair."

Fogarty gave a short nod and left the bloody room, muttering, "Creepy motherfucker," to himself.

"You have no idea," Gomez said to the empty room.

The door was still there, by the tire swing in the dark backyard. Pleased he'd finally caught a break, Gomez slipped through, checking his watch before he did so. He'd be back before midnight if his luck held.

When he reached the other side, and something rammed him in the lower back, he realized that counting on his luck holding was about as useful as hoping bleach would get out the blood stains in that carpet. Luck had no place here, no more than hope.

He rolled when he fell, avoiding the stampeding feet. Gomez lifted his head and struggled to his knees. In the dark, the retreating rump looked a lot like a rhinoceros, but you never could tell what may be rampaging in these parts. It was large, dense, and alive. He stayed that way, stunned, on his hands knees, for some time. He winced at the at the lump that rose on the back of his head.

Before he could get to his feet, a hand closed on the back of his jacket and lifted him up. His teeth snapped together as his rescuer put him on his feet. Gomez was about to thank the man who picked him up, but when he saw the shining mouth made of spinning gears, he lost all the spit in his mouth.

"Eloin Gomez, I have been looking for you."

"Officer Tock, it's a pleasure to see you. And surely you know if you need me, all you need to do is call. I'll come running," he said, his voice calm.

"Lies," he said, the sibilant S sounding like the constant tickticktick of a stopwatch. "I'm taking you in."

His uniform was far from clean; he must have been busy that night. Rhinoceros shit (it was a rhino after all) smeared on his left arm, and blood from a woman in the market had splattered across his scar. She had been trying to run from him, and he had caught her.

As Tock wrestled Gomez's arms behind him and prepared a set of barbed handcuffs, he said, "But Officer Tock, if you take me in, you will not catch that beast who befouled your uniform so heinously," he said, gesturing to the departing mass with his free hand. "Surely you want to catch it for trampling your deputy to death?"

"You are a much better catch," Officer Tock said. "We haven't forgotten the theft last month. Old Traitor Joe still cries at night, missing the broken promises you took from him."

Eloin had broken his promise to love me, to cherish me, to stay with me.

He gritted his teeth against the whispers coming from his pocket. As for Old Traitor Joe, Gomez had needed the promises to pay for a tricky solvent to remove the regret and blood stains from the concrete where a father had accidentally run over his toddler son. Gomez hadn't wanted to steal from the old man, but there had been no other option. He had hoped to return some broken promises to the old man. Someday.

But this time, he had no choice again. Regretting the necessity, with his free hand he slipped the girl's red vial from its pocket, and dropped it.

It shattered on the street and the air around them was filled with terror and pain, and an unwavering shriek. Officer Tock could withstand much, but he often was prepared for physical attacks. Few people unprepared could handle the tempest of a little girl's terror, and Officer Tock staggered back.

Gomez wrenched his hand free from Tock and took off, leaving the shrieks behind him, still assaulting the officer.

Now we add assaulting an officer. A most auspicious start to the evening, Gomez thought. If he'd ever be able to return to the Mad City, he'd better bring protection. He dashed into the heart of the city, looking for either a good hiding pace or the bazaar where he could lose himself in a crowd. The various stains on the streets and walls said their constant soliloquies to anyone who could hear: who had made them, how it had happened, and when. A particularly vibrant stain of brain and blood in an alley street whispered to him, encouraging him to approach.

Safe behind this door. Tried to get there before Tock got me. Safe here. Hide here.

Without question, Gomez wrenched the door open and dove inside. With his back to the door, he caught his breath, but tried to gauge his surroundings; his savior might be worse than his pursuer. It was pitch black, but he could hear the stains. They murmured to him, as if delighted to find an ear.

One cup of stock, not one pint, fuck you fuck you the beef blood the duck blood the wine and let's impress and woo and win—

The door through was this way, he finally gleaned. By feeling the counters and listening to the stains, he realized he was in a kitchen of some sort, one that had been abandoned by a mad cook.

Guided by the murmuring stains, he crept through the black

building until he got a hand on a doorknob. The door opened to a bustling, loud marketplace.

Sending a prayer of thanks to the Virgin, Gomez sighed audibly. He couldn't afford to take too much time. Tock knew Gomez would visit the market for supplies, so he would eventually end up here. He cast around for his target, and saw the bald head and scratchy robes three stalls down.

Father Brown had brown skin, brown robes, was of indeterminate age, and worshipped an indeterminate god. Gomez didn't ask many personal questions. Through trial and error, plus a scar on the back of his neck, he learned how not to offend the Father.

"Eloin the Bold!" the Father said, grinning broadly. "It is good to see you. How does your soul measure up today?"

"Fifteen children's' steps, Father," Gomez said. He still wasn't sure he understood all of the ways the Father measured souls, but he figured anything involving innocents was safe.

"Wonderful to hear. What can I do for you today? Are you looking to erase regret? Envy, perhaps?"

"More than that, I am afraid," he said. "Murderous violence mixed with a bit of sexual abuse. Pain, rage, fear, hatred."

Father Brown frowned and shook his head. "A shame. May the guilty rot between the teeth of Mother When."

Gomez winced, but didn't say anything. "I can offer a vial of rage and fear. Do you have anything for me?"

The Father shook his head, frowning. "I have the perfect thing for you, Eloin." He gestured to a glass bell that held a gray, papery beehive inside. "This hive of bees will devour all emotion in a room, thriving on pain and rage, but it's much more expensive than a vial of emotion."

Gomez pursed his lips. "I have a lock of hair from a dead girl."

The Father shook his head again. He glanced at the scarlet hankie meticulously folded in Gomez's pocket. "I will give you the hive for that."

Don't cast me off don't throw me away don't leave me behind—

"No deal," Gomez said automatically. "That's worth ten hives to me."

"Eloin," the Father said kindly. "Don't look at it like the worth of what you have versus the worth of what I have. Look at it that I am giving you the thing worth the most to me, and you're doing the same. I'm but a poor man of the cloth, while you are wealthy." His eyes flitted briefly to behind Gomez's shoulder. "I see Officer Tock has arrived. He looks very angry. I will throw in a key with the hive. Deal?"

A key. Now he was offering both the solution to Gomez' problem and a quick escape. He thought about where Tock would take him, what would happen to him.

Gomez swore in Spanish, a long string that questioned the Father's parentage and his sexual proclivities. Before the man could rescind his offer, he took the precious scrap of silk from his pocket and slammed it on the table.

Floor it get away get away get away no more Eloin no more love—

The Father passed over the glass bell and a key wrapped in a dirty piece of cotton. "Pleasure doing business," he said brightly.

"Fuck your grandmother," Gomez said, picking up his treasures. He turned and ran back to the door he had exited, noticing with surprise that it had been the home of the mad chef Patty Cake, who had cooked for kings. And cooked kings. He slipped the key and returned.

He could feel the regret and the pain leave him as he stepped through, and the guilt settled on him that he would be free of the weight.

I'm sorry, Miranda. Again.

Gomez checked his watch. 11:56. He slipped the key and the cotton into his pocket, then leaned against the brick wall and panted, free, for the moment, of the terrifying specter of the stopwatch faced man. The bees under the bell buzzed sleepily, and he peered in to look at them by the light of the street lamp. Like normal honeybees, they crawled around their hive. Unlike honeybees, they were black and white.

The front door of the murder scene was unlocked, but Gomez could see a squad car across the street, as usual. They didn't trust him fully, and they shouldn't.

Pulled by the words of pain and terror in the dining room, Gomez went straight there and placed the bell on the table. He took a deep breath, then lifted it. The bees came out, first in ones and twos, and then in an ever-growing cloud. Gomez stood stock still to watch.

The bees flew to the walls and floor, collecting the blood and other fluids like nectar, then returned to their hive. They came back out, and repeated this again. Within ten minutes, the dining room was stripped clean of the shit, blood, fluid, rage, hatred, and fear. The mother would never forget the son's murder, but the dining room would no longer be a terrifying reminder of it.

His pocket moved briefly, and he glanced down. Two bees were trying to get inside. Not wanting to get stung, he pulled it open for them, and they flew down and collected something, then flew back to their hive.

The memory as they flew by was fleeting, and he grasped it desperately. Miranda.

He'd broken her heart, ended their relationship. He said he had loved someone else, had said they couldn't be together. She had driven off in a crying rage and drove straight into a tree. He found her lying on the street, the car on top of the broken tree trunk. She had gone through the windshield. The blood had dribbled from her mouth, and he had dabbed it away gently as he had tried to urge her to hold on, and how fucking sorry he was.

It had been a lie. There was no one else, but Miranda was comfortably unaware of the horrors Gomez was becoming familiar with, and he hadn't wanted to share his nightmare with her. He would keep her ignorant. He would keep her safe.

Why Eloin, why? I love—

Then it was gone. Gomez was left with an empty, sad feeling, unsure of why he had felt that way. Something about a lost love. He gritted his teeth; the feeling was one he was familiar with.

All of the bees accounted for, he put the bell back over them, and tried to think of what all-night-diners were nearby. He needed coffee.

As he drove off in his black van, he wondered what kind of honey these bees made.

MUR LAFFERTY is an editor, podcaster, and author. She is the host of *Escape Pod* and *I Should Be Writing*, and the author of *Playing For Keeps* and *The Afterlife Series*. Online she can be found at *murverse.com*, and in real life she can be found in Durham, NC, but don't find her there, cause that's just creepy, yo.

DON'T CHEW YOUR FOOD

BY HARRY CONNOLLY

AS SOON AS OWEN KELLER SAW THE SNEAKER, he should have known. It was small, bright red, and the knotted lace had been cut instead of untied. He'd caught a sudden whiff of sour milk, wet wipes, and dust bunnies from it.

He should have known right then.

He stood on the street corner trying to get his bearings. This wasn't a dream; it had taken him a full hour, but he'd finally convinced himself that, whatever this place was, it was as real as his Upper East Side condo, the studio, or any of his restaurants.

An old man shuffled by him, smelling of cat food, stale garlic bread, and loneliness. God, the smells here were so strong, and so filled with weird associations. Sometimes it seemed Owen could smell their memories.

He leaned against a brick wall as a couple of wind-up cops walked past, their frozen grins turned toward him, then toward no one in particular. They smelled of mineral oil and broken bones. The wall rippled. From somewhere down the block, a group of kids started scream-laughing, but it was impossible to tell if they were playing, fighting, or both.

This was no good. Scents surrounded him, but he couldn't focus. The streetlights were so bright, and the sidewalks filled with creeps. A pair of old men in tails and top hats strutted by, loudly abusing their black servants. Coming the other way were a group of ten men—all hollow-eyed creeps with slicked back hair and skinny ties of the kind his father used to wear—advancing toward him with the hungry eyes of muggers.

Owen backed away from them, half-expecting one of them to backhand him like his father used to, but they looked him over and turned away, uninterested. A group of young girls in poodle skirts floated behind them, their hair standing straight up like bundled hay, their cloven feet gliding above the sidewalk.

The creeps and not-hallucinations kept distracting him from the task at hand. Their smells were so strong, but when he tried to sift through them for the scent he wanted, one of them would break his concentration with a leer, scowl, or predatory lick of the lips.

He glanced down the alley across the street. There was a fire escape down there, and although the buildings looked like upside down pyramids half sunk in the street—the roofs encroaching over the road so they nearly touched above—Owen was sure he could climb above the streetlights. Maybe he would be safer in the dark.

Every car on the road pulled to the curb to let a glass truck full of murky water pass by, and Owen took advantage of the lull in traffic to run to the mouth of the alley. His foot struck an empty plastic blister pack, and the noise it made echoed.

A woman stepped out from behind a Dumpster. "Who's there?" she shouted. Then she pointed a gun at him.

Owen stared in open-mouthed shock. A second person he couldn't really see bolted from beside the woman, running so fast down the alley that it was little more than a blur.

"No!" the woman cried, spinning to aim her pistol in the other direction but it was too late. The figure was gone.

Just as Owen belatedly thought it would be a good idea to duck out of sight beyond the mouth of the alley, the woman aimed her weapon at him again. "You." Her voice was low and dangerous. "Tubby. Come here."

There was no arguing with a woman holding a gun. Owen showed his empty hands and shuffled forward. The stink of rotting garbage washed over him and he staggered but didn't fall. "I'm sorry," he said.

"You sad son of a bitch. You're Awake, aren't you?" She looked Vietnamese but her accent was pure South Jersey. Her nose had been broken and never reset, and she had three scars running parallel across her face. She looked to be in her mid-thirties, but her hair was as white as a ghost's. The dark circles under her eyes made her look more tired than him. "Look at you."

Owen did as he was told. He wore a heavy white chef jacket stretched over his belly, striped pants, and orange crocks over wool socks. They were work clothes, and they weren't meant to impress. He didn't need clothes for that, in his world.

The breeze shifted and he could smell her—gun oil, sore-muscle cream, and lightning-hot anxiety. "I didn't mean to interrupt—"

"Shut the fuck up. Do you know how long I've been chasing that Shameful? I'm trying to think of a reason not to waste a bullet on you."

"I can help you!" Owen blurted out. "I can help you find it again."

She hesitated, then lowered her weapon, stepping back to let him step into the place the—what had she called it? A Shameful?—had been. It was a swirl of awful smells, but Owen's nose found the one he wanted quickly. He'd always had a sensitive nose, but in this strange place, he could track like a bloodhound.

What's more, he could smell the thing—he knew instantly that this wasn't a human being he was smelling. It was something much more and much less—another not-hallucination. In this insane city, he could actually smell its shame. The trail stood out like a neon light.

"I can track it," he said, "but you have to help me in return."

"Not killing you immediately is my best offer."

"Fuck that," Owen said, although her gun made his guts watery. "Kill me and you'll have to start all over again. Trade with me and I'll lead you to it right now. And all I want is your help in finding something."

"And what's that?"

"A green door with two dragons on it, facing each other."

She was no poker player; her expression made it clear that she knew the place. "It's a deal."

He followed the scent into the next street. Buildings here were angled so steeply over the road that he had to duck low to avoid bumping his head on the window sills. The trail led through a basement door that inexplicably opened onto a rooftop somewhere, then down the gigantic broken marble forearm of a statue, then into a burned out bakery.

"In there," Owen said, standing at the edge of a dirt lot. "I can smell it, whatever it is, crouching inside. I can smell it breathing."

"You have super smell? Here?" She gave him a pitying look.

"I've always been sensitive—wait!" he hissed as she advanced toward the house. "What if it's a trap?"

Gun drawn, she slipped inside. Owen felt a sudden stench of fear and shame wash over him, and the gunfire started.

Without thinking, Owen jumped to his feet. He tried to think of a safe place he could run to, and that moment's indecision was too much.

Two figures leapt over a second floor balcony and struck the ground running like streaks. One of them, wrapped in brown robes and green garbage bags, collided with him.

Owen hit the sidewalk hard, and the robed thing fell partly on top of him. The hood of its robe fell back, exposing its face.

It was horrible. The Shameful had a face like a rotting pear. Its cheeks and forehead were covered with weeping sores, and its bulging, panicked eyes rolled crazily. "You saw me!" It bellowed. Then it laid a meaty hand on Owen's chest.

Owen tried to roll away, but the creature was powerful enough to pin him in place.

"You saw me!" It bellowed again in a dullard's voice. It lifted itself onto his chest and, with its other hand, drew out a long boning knife. "Can't let you tell." Owen grabbed its wrist with both hands, but it was strong. The dirty tip of the knife moved toward his mouth. "Take your tongue. Can't let you tell."

The stink of it was so strong he gasped, and then the knife was in his mouth. He bit down on the blade, hoping to trap it, but he knew it was hopeless. He was about to be maimed—killed—by a fucking monster in a crazy dream city; it didn't make any sense—

He bit down as hard as he could, and the knife blade shattered. The Shameful looked as shocked as Owen felt, and it pulled its hand back to examine the ruined weapon.

A gunshot tore through its shoulder and it collapsed to the side. Owen rolled out from beneath it, spitting out sharp pieces of the knife.

The white-haired woman held her gun on the wounded creature. "Let's try this again," she said. She raised an old-fashioned Polaroid camera in her other hand, and snapped a picture.

"NO!" The Shameful screamed, its misery real and potent.

The woman was unimpressed. "Yes! Do you want this?" she pulled out the undeveloped picture with her teeth, threw the camera aside, then held the photo up. "You can have it! But first you have to tell me where my mother is!"

Owen backed away. Whatever she was doing, it had nothing to do with him, and he wanted as much space between them as he could get while keeping her in sight. It took him a moment to remember that he had a knife of his own, his best Wusthof, hidden under his shirt, but he hadn't brought it for fighting. After less than a minute of talking with the creature, the woman dropped the photo onto its chest then shot it in the head.

"My turn," Owen said to her as she jogged toward him.

"I know," she snapped. "Shut up and follow me."

She led him through an alley into a public gym. Behind the front desk was a wall of mirrors, each of which reflected a different image. She grabbed Owen by the elbow and pulled him through one. They ended up in a darkened, empty movie theater. The woman led him up to the balcony.

"It don't understand," Owen said. "It tried to stab me with a knife made out of... hard candy or something. Or thin ceramic. It was unbelievably brittle. Everything in this city is wrong."

The woman gave him an odd look. "I'm Gina."

"I'm Owen Keller."

"Christ, I knew I recognized you from somewhere. You're that guy on that cooking show!"

"Wrong," Owen said. "I'm that guy on *the* cooking show."

"Don't get all arrogant with me," Gina said. "Not in this place."

Owen shrugged. She was probably right. "I'm sorry about your mother. I hope she's going to be okay."

"No chance of that. But maybe, if I make the right deal, I can get her out of here in not too many pieces. So, what's keeping you awake?"

"A job." Owen didn't want to talk about it, but in that moment it was irresistible. It had been *days* and he couldn't talk to anyone about this—not even Roscoe—without risking everything. "I do private parties sometimes, and my fee is huge. As it should be. But this time... I let them bring me blindfolded to the kitchen. I let them bring me the food I was supposed to prepare—they didn't tell me..." He thought of that tiny red sneaker again, lying in the doorway, and he realized he didn't really want to talk about it after all.

"Okay," Gina said. "I can guess the rest."

"I have to find out who it was," Owen said. The words wouldn't stay inside of him. "I have to know."

"Well, even if I was in the market for a noob to train, I wouldn't take you. You're too fat and you think too slow. I wouldn't bet a dollar on you to last the night." She stood. "Sit tight. We're going to hole up here for a little while, until the Shamefuls forget us. After a bit I'm going to go out to make sure. I'll be back for you, don't worry."

"I'm too damn tired to worry," Owen said. He walked up the rake of the balcony aisle. He stood beside a broken section of the wall, letting the air from outside wash over him. Thousands of scents entered him, and he closed his eyes to sort them. The unwashed knife was under his jacket in case he needed to refresh his memory, but he didn't need it. He did the uninterrupted work he'd tried to do on the street corner.

He didn't think about what Gina had said about surviving the night. He didn't think about how close he'd come to having his tongue cut out. He didn't think about how long he'd smelled that smell the very first night he'd came here, for a private job that had paid in solid gold, when he should have known what he was slicing and roasting.

There it was. The scent.

He was so excited he nearly cried out. Gina hadn't returned so there was no one to tell. He rushed down the stairs to the nearest exit.

The street was more crowded now. He oriented himself to the direction that the wind was blowing and there was the scent of that tiny shoe, and the cut of meat he'd prepared. He followed the trail for ten harrowing blocks, but everyone around him, even the things that were clearly not human, seemed jumpy and nervous. Finally, he came to a city park—which looked like it had been constructed on the site of a meteor strike—and down inside the crater was a vast flea market.

The scent led down there, and Owen couldn't quit now. A long set of concrete stairs sat to his left, but the crowds making their way up or down were crammed together and moving so slowly they were practically standing still. Owen stepped over the edge of the crater and slid down the loose dirt toward the outer circle of stalls.

It was like jumping into a lake of stench. Below the rim of the crater, the breezes couldn't stir the scents, and they lingered, mixed and concentrated. Owen could smell the joys and miseries attached to old lipstick nubs, VHS copies of kung fu videos, cracked coffee thermoses, spent bullet casings, rusted camp stoves, and ten thousand other objects. He reeled as his momentum carried him deeper into it, and it was so powerful he nearly shut his eyes and collapsed.

Not here. Even he knew better than to close his eyes in a place like this. Owen opened his jacket, drew the knife partway, then pressed it to his nose. He could smell that same smell again, and as he slid the knife back under his jacket he found the trail again.

It was the shoe. The same shoe. He found it in a stall near the center, in a jumble of discarded junk. "Where did you get this?"

The stall's proprietor was barely more than skin stretched over bone. It smiled widely, revealing 50 or 60 long yellow teeth, and said: "Oh no, sir. We don't do provenance here. No coin, either. Barter only."

Useless. Owen picked up the shoe and took a deep whiff. He could smell the sweat of climbing, plastic building blocks, and the dust of a baseball field. It wasn't like sight, but he would recognize that boy again as easily as if he'd studied a photo of him. He put the shoe back.

"THIEF!" the proprietor screamed. "You stole from me!"

Owen stepped back in panic. "No, I—" He bumped into a figure behind him and fell into the mud. It was one of the wind-up cops. It clamped a hand on his wrist, its frozen smile chilling.

"Officer, he stole memories from my merchandise—"

Owen drew his chef's knife. The cop might have had a key in its back, but it felt like flesh. Maybe a quick slash—

"What's this?" the proprietor said, snatching the knife out of his grip as though he was a child. The proprietor held the knife up to its ear, then examined the edge. Something made it very happy, because it smiled and said: "What have you been slicing with this, hmm?"

It pulled open its shirt, revealing a set of balance scales where its heart and lungs should have been. It placed the blade on one side and the shoe on the other. The blade was heavier.

"This will do for a trade," it said, "And more. Would you like to choose another item?"

"No," Owen said, standing. That knife was a gift from his father, and it had almost been a sign of approval. But the cop had his arm and he wouldn't risk his life for it. "I want the provenance."

The proprietor bowed. "I traded for it from a woman with a mop for a leg and vinegar eyes. That is all I can tell you." The side of the scale with the shoe seemed to grow heavier until they were almost balanced. The cop released him.

Owen took the shoe and ran like hell. The crater was too steep to climb out, so he had to suffer the interminable delay of the stairs. Someone stole the shoe from his pocket in the press of bodies, and he was too frightened to make a fuss. Back on the street, it seemed that everything had changed, but he was able to follow his own scent trail of helpless shame and terror back to the theater.

Gina still hadn't returned. Or she had returned and, finding him gone, had left. He sat helpless and miserable for nearly an hour until she slipped in through a side door. "It's time," Gina called.

He joined her. "Is it far?"

"No," Gina said, "But listen. You follow me from a distance, at least fifteen feet. I will lead you past the door and I will glance up at it. You'll know the door and I'll keep walking. Capishe?" She cracked the door open a few inches, peered through, and gasped. She held still so Owen did, too. The sound of crinkling paper came from outside, but he didn't know what it meant.

Eventually, it faded. "My parents owned a cheesesteak place," she said, almost as though testing the effect her voice would have. "That's probably way beneath you."

"I love cheesesteak," Owen answered. The memory of that shoe came back to him so powerfully that he flinched. "I eat everything."

The crinkling paper sound didn't come back. Gina slipped into the alley. Owen followed her at a slower pace, letting her get some distance. Eventually, they were back on the street, weaving between newspaper sellers, old women pushing shopping carts fully of gray sludge, and other stranger sights.

It was two blocks before Gina turned her head and looked up at a building. When he reached it, Owen glanced up, too. It was the right door—painted green, with two dragons baring their teeth at each other.

He turned around and looked at the building across the street. There it was. That was the place he'd been brought to cook that damn meal, and there was the window he'd looked through when he'd seen the dragon door. He crossed toward it.

The windows weren't barred, but he wasn't fit enough to climb through one. He rang the doorbell.

The door was opened by a young man with a missing ear and the fear-stink of penned cattle. His left leg was missing below the hip, and he had a mop in its place. A wave of antiseptic billowed through the doorway. The young man barely looked at him. "You're expected." He led Owen into the building.

They went down a long hall into a sitting room. Every surface, even the chairs and desk, were tiled like an operating room. Two women worked in the far corner of the room. Both of their right legs had been sawed off and replaced with mops, and their left hands had been replaced with stained kitchen rags. Owen had a sudden sickening feeling he knew how they'd lost those limbs.

The door at the far end of the room opened and a not-hallucination strolled in. It was tall and lanky with a misshapen head and goggly eyes. It was dressed in a dark, sober waistcoat and tie, but it moved like a boy on Christmas morning. "Mr. Keller!" it exclaimed. "How pleased I am! We didn't speak on the occasion of your previous visit, but let me assure you that my guests and I were delighted by the meal you prepared!"

It smiled; its teeth were metal-bright, rounded and serrated like the tips of steak knives. To his own disgust, Owen heard himself say: "Thank you."

"There wasn't a problem with the payment, I hope?"

"I'm not here about the payment," Owen said. He wanted to bolt for the door. What had he been thinking? What had he imagined he would do when he got here? Bad enough he had prepared that meal, but coming here now was madness.

The thing stepped very close to him, as if sensing his instinct to flee. "My name is Mr. Savor. Please! Sit!"

Mr. Savor raised its hands as if it was about to push him into a ceramic chair, but Owen dropped into it on his own. In place of fingers, Mr. Savor had forks, tiny knives, and delicate silver spoons.

"So, Mr. Keller, I'm sure you get this sort of thing all the time and I hope you don't mind, but I consider myself something of a gourmand." Mr. Savor leaned against the desk, looming over Owen. "Not that I would compare my humble self to you! Your reputation is flawless! But in my own way I try to keep current and eat only the finest. I'm sure you understand."

Sweat ran down Owen's face. He couldn't look away from those teeth. He was going to die here. He was utterly certain of it. "What matters is that you enjoy what you eat."

"Oh, quite!" Mr. Savor leaned close, his voice low and conspiratorial. "But I must ask you, as an expert: What is going to be the next big thing?"

"T- t- terrines."

Mr. Savor was disappointed. "I thought terrines were two years ago."

"Everything is two years ago." Owen's voice trembled. "Everything is being done somewhere by someone. Savory chocolate sauce? Pork chops and oysters? Sri Lankan curry? Someone is doing that right now, and you, being somewhat plugged in, have heard about it. But you're asking what's going to break out to the people who *aren't* plugged in, and I'm saying terrines."

"What makes you think so?"

"Because," Owen said, trying to take control of his fear, "I've already shot three fucking episodes on them for the fall."

Mr. Savor laughed with delight, but Owen didn't find anything reassuring in the sound.

"I came here because I have to know—"

The door behind him swung open. "My friends!" Mr. Savor said as it stood.

Three horrors entered the room. The first was tiny, hunch-backed and gray like an old woman. It wore huge tinted drug store sunglasses that looked like safety goggles. Its face and canary yellow smock were both spattered with food, splashes of blood, and old sweat stains. As it shuffled in, a long hairy tongue slid from its mouth and licked a greenish smear from its chin.

The second was huge, bald and pink, and so fat that it had to be carried on the shoulders four men. Each of its fingers ended in an iron skewer and its dainty feet were a foot off the ground. It smiled at Mr. Savor as though their meeting was a surprise.

The third looked like a middle-aged woman with rumpled clothes and frazzled hair. Her eyes were wide and staring, and as soon as she saw Owen, her mouth fell open and her lips curled back, revealing teeth like sharpened, slow-turning gears.

The worst one of all came last. It was Gina.

"Owen Keller, celebrity chef and restaurateur," Mr. Savor said, "Let me introduce my guests: Miss Indulgence, Mr. Appetite, and Miss Bite. We were the lucky four to enjoy the meal you prepared."

"And now you're back with us again," Miss Bite said, her gaze focused and hungry.

The smell of them was overwhelming. Owen wished he could shut it off, but he didn't have the nerve to pinch his nose in front of them.

But Gina... He was already so damn tired, and discovering she had sold him out nearly broke him. A glance at the door Mr. Savor had entered showed that the two mop women were cleaning in front of it. Would they block him if he tried to run? He wanted to collapse from despair.

"Mr. Keller, what's going to be the next big thing?" Mr. Appetite asked.

Mr. Savor interjected: "That was my very first question! His answer was quite illuminating."

"You can discuss it over dinner," Gina said, stepping forward. "My payment."

"Of course," Mr. Savor answered. It went around the desk, slid open a tiled drawer, and took out a sheet of parchment. "Your letter of introduction."

Gina opened it and glanced at the contents. Satisfied, she nodded at Mr. Savor.

Miss Indulgence stared from behind its dark glasses. "Time for another feast, I think."

"Yes," Mr. Appetite said. "You've outdone yourself this time, Mr. Savor."

"Wait," Owen said, mind racing. "You haven't told me what I came here to find out." The four creatures stared at him, waiting. "The night I cooked for you, I... I know it was a child that I served. A boy."

"Yes?" Mr. Savor prompted.

Was this question worth dying for? Not that he had a choice anymore. "Who was he? Where did he come from? I— I want to meet his parents."

One of the mop women caught Owen's attention by looking up at him sharply. At the same time, Mr. Savor said: "Why, he was my son, of course!" Owen found that he couldn't look away from the cleaning woman; the expression on her face was empty, intense, and completely horrifying. Her eyes were the same color as extravecchio balsamic. "You don't think I'd eat just *anything*, do you? I like to have some idea where my food comes from."

"Besides," Mr. Appetite said. "We can't keep eating each other." It tugged its housecoat open to reveal a clumsily-stitched slash in its left breast. Something that looked like brown gravy seeped out.

"This isn't just meat to us," Miss Bite said. "It's experience and memory, too. When we ate that boy, we experienced the thrill of climbing a tree, of running through tall grass, of cowering below the covers as mysterious shapes moved in the closet."

"All carefully nurtured by me!" Mr. Savor said.

"And quite wonderfully, too," Mr. Appetite said.

Miss Indulgence frowned. "I thought the running was a bit gamey."

"Oh dear," Mr. Appetite said. "I fear for your palate, dear lady."

"But you will be a special treat, Mr. Keller," Miss Bite said. She hadn't looked away from him, like a snake hypnotizing a mouse.

"When we eat you, we'll experience every fine meal you've ever had: duck confit, foie gras, everything."

"Me?" Owen said. "You don't want me. I've never been careful about what I eat. Grubby diner eggs and lunch truck chili and supermarket hot dogs with relish from the public condiment dispenser..." He looked around at the carefully scrubbed and gleaming tiles around him. "Those are the experiences you'd get from me."

The four not-hallucinations seemed confused and discomfited. For a moment, Owen thought they might let him go.

"I guess," Mr. Savor said, "if the great Owen Keller is catholic in his tastes, we should be too."

One of the men supporting Mr. Appetite grabbed Owen's wrist in a powerful grip. Owen shrieked, the stink of his own fear flooding his nostrils.

"This isn't what we agreed," Gina said.

Mr. Savor bowed and Owen was released. Gina came forward and aimed the gun at him.

"I'm disappointed, Mr. Savor," Miss Bite said. "We're not going to have Terror of Being Sliced Apart."

"We always have Terror of Being Sliced Apart," Miss Indulgence said.

"Because it's so goooooood."

"You'll have to settle for Despair Before Being Shot To Death," Gina said. That seemed to mollify them, and Gina held up a water bottle. "Take a big swig and hold it in your mouth. For insurance." Owen only stared at her. "No? Look, the last noob as clueless as you was tortured to death in District 13. It took him months to die. I'm going to save you that pain. I'm very good with this gun; I can do it so you won't feel a thing." She put the gun to Owen's lips and he opened his mouth. "See? I'm doing you a favor, and this deal is going to help my mother."

Crazy. The whole world had gone crazy, and so had he. Owen felt a vicious hunger pang, and he had an absurd urge to request a last meal, and just as he felt like bursting out in laughter, he bit down on the gun.

His teeth sheared through the barrel like a ripe apple.

Gina, shocked, jumped back. Owen had only taken the end of the barrel, but it slid down his throat like pudding. She aimed the gun again and he lunged for it, still hungry. The bullet she fired went into his mouth—it should have blasted out the back of his head, but instead it vanished into him. He bit down on her gun again and she barely managed to yank her hand away to save her own fingers.

She stumbled back, weaponless, her eyes wide and as full of madness as his own. "Don't make me call the surgeons," she whispered. "Don't make me."

Owen chewed on the gun and felt it slide into his belly. "Get out of here."

He turned. Miss Bite leaned forward like a predator about to spring. As it leapt Owen did, too. His mouth gaped impossibly wide, taking one of its arms between his jaws. It tried to pull away at the last moment, but he bit down, severing its arm between the elbow and shoulder. Miss Bite screamed and, twisting wildly, fell onto its stomach.

Owen lunged at the back of its head, opening his mouth as wide as he could. His teeth gouged through the tile floor, bursting the ceramic and rotted wood beneath as he bit away the upper half of its body.

The hole in the floor was large enough to jump through, but Owen couldn't run away, not when he was *starving*. He gulped down the rest of Miss Bite, taking in more broken tile and shattered furniture, but none of it satisfied him. Everything he swallowed turned into more hunger.

The other three horrors were scrambling for the exit. Owen opened his mouth as wide as a door, then even wider; he felt his hunger catch them, dragging them into his gaping jaws.

His lips were stretched so tight he thought they would tear like threadbare fabric, and his eyes felt as though they would burst like squashed grapes. But his nostrils were wide, and he could smell the utter terror and helplessness of the three horrors, and the bursting caulk of the shattered tiles, and the splintered wooden beams, and dusty bricks.

The creatures fell into him and were destroyed, but he couldn't stop. The walls collapsed, the floors were flung up and the roof thrown down as the matter near him tore itself into dust and flowed into his throat.

His mouth widened further and the pull became stronger. The wind and air fell into him, and fire, and fear, and a thousand thousand pieces of trash from out on the street, with all their small, useless memories. He felt people plummet into him, but it wasn't just their flesh he consumed; it was also their love, their regret, their hope, their desperate, pathetic need for kindness. The whole awful city flew into pieces and was sucked down into his guts like a house of cards in a tornado. And with it he devoured all connection, all sense, all wildness.

Still his hunger grew, and he ate distance, time, then nothingness itself.

His hunger burned, but there was nothing left for him to take in except self, and slowly, he dwindled.

But the city, whatever it was and whatever had created it, could not simply be destroyed. Not in his way. He felt a strange unfolding in the depths of his hunger, and the nightmarish city recreated itself, and recreated him, too.

Owen collapsed into the rubble, cutting his palms against broken bricks. The awful odors of the city had returned and he was himself again, down to his stupid crocs.

He scrambled out of the second crater he'd seen that day. At least Mr. Savor and his friends—and their whole city block—had been destroyed. He crawled onto the asphalt, not sure if he was even real, or what real might possibly mean.

Gina stood at the end of the street, staring at him in abject terror, and god, how hungry he was for it.

HARRY CONNOLLY lives in Seattle with his beloved wife, his beloved son, and his beloved library system. You can find him online at: *www.harryjconnolly.com*

SPIRIT OF THE CENTURY™ PRESENTS...

A new line of pulp-era fiction! Talking apes, flying jet-men, and scrappy gadgeteering gals abound! Be on the look-out in the coming months for the following new titles in softcover and ebook, from **Evil Hat Productions!**

The *Dinocalypse Trilogy*, from author **Chuck Wendig:**
  Dinocalypse Now (ISBN 978-1-61317-003-8)
  Beyond Dinocalypse (ISBN 978-1-61317-016-8)
  Dinocalypse Forever (ISBN 978-1-61317-017-5)

King Khan by **Harry Connolly** (ISBN 978-1-61317-018-2)

Khan of Mars by **Stephen Blackmoore** (ISBN 978-1-61317-019-9)

... As well as new novels by *Atomic Robo* scribe **Brian Clevinger** and *Urban Shaman* author **C. E. Murphy!**

On sale soon from www.evilhat.com, as well as an online or brick & mortar bookstore near you!